RADIATION DISASTER

The abrasions on Jean's flushed face stood out angrily. As Rule bent down and touched her head, something hideous happened. His fingers caught in a few strands of her hair, and they came away in his hand. In spite of the cool air and the dampness, her skin burned to his touch.

"She has radiation sickness," he said.

"What chance has she got?" Rendrick asked.

"I don't know enough for sure. I've read that tufts of hair coming out and high temperature are early symptoms. But look at those cuts on her face—even the small ones aren't healing well."

"We could be in port in Israel by tonight," Rendrick said. "She could be in hospital in Tel Aviv within hours."

But suddenly disaster struck; the small boat heeled far over, and the anchor rope twanged and broke. Rendrick made a dive for the helm, but he was too late. The tiller banged over to its fullest starboard reach, then crashed back again as the rudder swung uselessly to and fro. Water cascaded over the gunwale. Then the boat capsized, and the violent waves smashed over the half-submerged hull in clouds of spray . . .

HOSTAGE

by COLIN MASON

PINNACLE BOOKS • NEW YORK CITY

This is a work of fiction. All the characters and events portrayed in this book are fictional, and any resemblance to real people or incidents is purely coincidental.

HOSTAGE

HOSTAGE

One

The car with the army driver stopped at the kerb. A rear door opened and the general, a stocky, balding man with a black patch over his left eye, stepped to the pavement. People walking past on Dizengoff Street glanced at him with affection, for the general was a talisman to his people, the mere fact of his existence diminishing the threat of the hostile world around.

He moved briskly away from the car, his whole fabric exuding confidence, ability, toughness. Then, grotesquely, he hesitated in mid-step, his alert expression faded, his upright carriage slumped.

At that moment at least twenty bystanders were watching him, and several of these afterwards claimed they had known what was happening even before the sound of the shot reached them.

Blood seeped darkly through the back of the general's uniform. People hurried towards him. The car door opened again and two aides caught the general as he fell. He looked up weakly, but could not speak.

A small crowd gathered. Soon police and ambulance sirens began to wail.

" . . . all hell to pay," David Blackman, a thin, ageing diplomat, said into his telephone in Whitehall. "The Israeli defence minister's been shot. What? Oh

, from some considerable dis-
.estward, towards the port, there
.ses up that end. It's the easy way,
. Public figure, movements predicta-
...kes one shot with a first-class gun and
tele.. ..ghts. Plenty of time to get away. I doubt
they'l ..r find out who did it."

The brigadier on the other end of the line, who was also a member of the prime minister's advisory committee on the Middle East, asked: "Will the ceasefire get past this?"

"That's why it's all so crazy," Blackman said petulantly. "You know that at our last meeting we thought the chances for a peace settlement that'd stick were better than at any time in the past. That's no longer the case. The Israeli radio's howling for blood. They blame the Arabs, but I can't see what could have brought this on, as an officially sanctioned Arab policy, I mean, at this time, when everything's been sweetness and light. Nothing could be more provocative, and we must assume whoever did it meant it that way."

"It'll be some wild-eyed mob, even farther out and less responsible than Al Fatah," the brigadier commented. "The *fedayeen* are spawning them in scores."

"Just like the bloody Arabs, they're always going headlong into something like this, without giving a damn about what happens next. Well, the fact is the P.M. does want to know what comes next, so we're to peer into our glass ball, then tell him. The meeting's at half-past—that's in forty minutes from now. Please be prompt, that's a good chap," said Blackman, who had a large, now grown-up family, and tended to talk to everyone as if they were children. He hesitated, then added as an afterthought:

"There's another disturbing side to this. No time to

tell you about it now. It'll come up at the meeting, in fact it's the main thing we have to discuss. Relative to it, bring along anything you have, will you, on the capability of the American STM17? 'Bye."

He put down the telephone and, after a brief pause, began to dial another number.

"You shouldn't do it like that, Sir David," his secretary, who was new, pretty, and intimidating, reproved him. "Dial with the end of a pencil, I mean. The post office people say it causes a thousand wrong numbers every year. Use your finger."

"What's that? Oh, well, since you say so . . ." and he continued to dial the secret number, awkwardly, with his index finger.

The military attaché at the British Embassy in Cairo, Michael Rule, looked speculatively at his companion, Corinne Sampson, and wondered how quickly he would be able to get what he wanted from her, and what it might cost. She was a local reporter—a "stringer," in the jargon of the trade for the *Daily Feature*'s foreign correspondent, but according to Rule's sources, she didn't make enough money to live on out of that. She was nearly always broke, and that would obviously help.

They were sitting at a minute table, well away from any other, in Seventh Heaven, one of the small dimly lighted bars on Sharia al Gumhuria, a main street of Cairo. Here, due to the economical recycling of the same air through the conditioner, the atmosphere was always stale and heavy with the reek of spirits and tobacco smoke.

When Corinne began to laugh, Rule glanced uneasily about him, seeing no immediate cause for mirth.

"What's the joke?"

"Listen."

3

"But to what?"

"As if anyone could hear much in this place except that band."

"The band? Yes. Noisy, aren't they?"

"I meant the tune."

Rule turned his attention unwillingly to the racket, unable to see why it mattered, and finally recognised the abortive but vaguely familiar and still rollicking snatches of melody.

"Good Lord," he said. "They can't know. It is Rule Britannia, isn't it?"

They both laughed, and the tension that had built up between them relaxed.

"Now," Corinne said. "Come along with it. I can see you're in a hurry—so am I. Try not to be tactful and diplomatic."

Seeing her glass was empty he called over the waiter and bought some more of the pale pink fizzy drink, based on gin.

"It's about Abu Sharaf," he said.

"Abbie? Well, what?"

"We know the more obvious things. He's a Ph.D. in economics, lectures at the university, seems rich, throws his money around more than one would like to see in an economist. Apparently well in with the government, certainly has quite a few friends in important places, particularly the army. Likes foreign women and is especially partial to English girls. You're the current one."

Her gaze shifted.

"Actually things are pretty much over between me and Abbie. I think my lease there has finished—Abbie's always been one for variety where girls are concerned. You're asking me to sell him out in some way . . . ?"

"It isn't really that."

"Isn't it? Well, since you say so, I'd just as soon

believe you. This is a lousy country," she added, with apparent inconsequence. "Hot. Too much sand. Too many flies. Messy."

"You don't have to stay."

"I don't want to. I'd get out tomorrow if I could."

"And where would you go?"

"East west, home's best. London. I'm homesick, homesick as hell."

He nodded slowly.

"That's all right. We can do it. Passport, exit permit, passage paid, the lot—and all the other difficulties that've been keeping you away. All fixed. Tomorrow if you like."

The smile left her face, which had become sullen. She looks older, he thought, much closer to her real age.

"I'd have to get some money."

"Naturally. Shall we say a thousand, payable in London?"

"It's not enough. I'd need more than that. What about two thousand?"

"No."

"I'm not a fool. I can see you're after something important about Abbie. It ought to be worth two thousand, shouldn't it? That's not much these days."

"If you don't take this offer," he said softly. "You'll never get back to England. We won't help you again."

"As if you gave a damn what happens to me," she replied contemptuously. The band suddenly stopped playing and the resultant silence shouted, as they sat looking at one another.

Rule thought of the people waiting back at the embassy—the first secretary, the cipher clerk, the teleprinter girl. He glanced at his watch. The meeting in London would have started.

"Yes, time is getting on," she said, noticing his

involuntary movement and coming to a sudden decision. "I have a lot to do. Why not call me when things are more on the go?"

She rose and picked up her bag from the table. Her eyes were hard and her jaw was set. He could see she meant it, and conceded defeat with a gesture.

"Sit down. I can make it fifteen hundred. Not more."

"All right then. I shan't haggle."

"I've got to think of the taxpayers."

"To hell with the taxpayers. What do you want?"

"I want to talk about the Smirnoff's party. You were there, of course."

"So it was that," she replied, without looking at him. "I didn't even know you were there until I looked around, and you were watching me. You'd been listening in, hadn't you?"

"You could put it in a nicer way."

"I shan't bother. I'd been talking about Abbie?"

"You'd had several too many, I suppose—in fact you were rotten drunk and rather loud. It was lucky the whole party was just as loud. Nobody took much notice of you, except for me, that is."

"What had I said that was so interesting to you?"

"Something rather dangerous. You said you knew that Abu Sharaf was really a Jew."

"Lots of people are Jews."

"And is he?"

She lowered her eyes.

"Yes."

Rule felt the tension fade in his body and mind, his whole being relax.

"How do you know?"

"Abbie keeps a boat, a fast plushy one, called the *Miranda*. She's anchored at Port Said."

"Port Said? Why not Alex?"

"I'd wondered about that myself. I asked him once, and he said he liked to cruise about Manzala

Lake. Anyway, most of this year I went out with him, oh, quite a few weekends. Quite a few. That stopped a month or so ago.

"Several times when we were out at sea, late at night, I heard him get up. He thought I was asleep, but I was playing 'possum. There's a door in one wall of the main stateroom I'd thought just led into a cupboard, but it doesn't. There's a little room with a radio. Abbie was talking, then listening, to someone. It was quiet, and even though he wasn't talking loudly, I could tell it was Yiddish he was speaking. I can't talk it, but I know it when I hear it. Now why do you think he should be doing that, late at night, talking Yiddish to someone on that radio nobody was supposed to know about?"

Rule answered carefully:

"He doesn't have to be an Israeli, just because he can speak Yiddish."

"There are other things," she said, without looking at him. "Some small things, some rather funny, but they add up."

"I see."

"And anyway, you must have had an idea. You wouldn't have taken so much notice, like that, of what I'd said at the party, to be worth all this trouble, and the money, unless you knew something already."

He looked up quickly.

"Now about these talks on the radio . . . you said you couldn't understand a word. He never spoke in English?"

"Not while I could hear. And I couldn't tell, of course, what he was talking about, or who to . . . although I think maybe I know a bit about who . . . you see, Abbie mentioned his name quite a few times."

"His name?"

"Just the first name, but it came up three or four

times . . . rather odd when you think of it, that he should say it so much. Still, there are people like that, aren't there? They can hardly say a thing without repeating your name—Corinne this, Corinne that—"

"And what was the name Sharaf mentioned?"

"Jacob."

Rule looked at her silently, and got up.

"I say, is that all?" she asked anxiously. "Not that there's anything else I can think of. Doesn't seem much for fifteen hundred really, does it?"

Dusk in London fell on a dull, sleety day, cold enough for snow, although only odd flakes reached the pavements.

David Blackman was looking out of his office window at the drab evening sky when a knock came at his door. He glanced at his watch. It was twenty-five past four.

"Come on in, John," he called out.

"How did you know it was me?" Grimwade asked.

Blackman glanced at him curiously.

"Don't you know? It's because you're always first—always here three or four minutes before the due time of a meeting. I can't see why, but nobody else ever is these days."

"That's so," Grimwade agreed, a little startled. "I'd never really thought about it. Am I a nuisance, being like that?"

"Not a bit. Far from it. Like to see you."

But Grimwade could see that Blackman, who was convener and chairman of the Middle East advisory committee, had only the surface of his mind on the conversation. So he sat down quietly at the table, leaving Blackman to his thoughts. One by one the others came in, until all seven were present. Only then did Blackman turn away from the window and take his place at the head of the table.

"Most of you know already what there is to know about the assassination. The first reactions have been predictable. The Israeli press is yelling for action, and there's been a rumour—probably untrue—that the first air strikes against the Arab Republic have already taken off.

"However," and he smiled bleakly, "I don't think the Russian SAM3 missile defences will permit much activity of that sort. Our appreciation is that Cairo is quite safe from air attack.

"As you'll know, we've discussed this point a good deal at previous meetings and reported to the P.M., I believe accurately, that the one thing that'd take the stomach out of the Arabs so far as war with Israel is concerned would be a major hit at Cairo. That's why the Soviets have gone to so much trouble and expense over the city's defences.

"So the Russians think the way we do, and it would seem much Israeli opinion does too. Indeed the defence minister himself regarded Egypt as the only important enemy. He is on record as saying to a gathering of reserve officers, 'Egypt, and no other country, will be the one to launch an all-out war.' This is why the Israelis lash out with the repeated ground attacks and air raids designed specifically to hurt the Egyptian people—what they so nicely called the anticipatory counter-attack. The truth is, of course, that the war with Israel hasn't meant much to the average Egyptian. Not yet. The Cairo *fellaheen* haven't suffered personally.

"It was to prevent this, to remove the power of the Israeli Air Force to strike at Cairo in particular, that the Russians put in their missile batteries. And, in any realistic terms, the installation of those SAMs resulted in a ceasefire. So, if you'll bear with me a little longer, we come to the situation that's appeared to stand ever since."

He looked silently down the table for a few seconds, then asked:

"Could Cairo be hurt seriously in any other way? What do we think?"

The brigadier, near the foot of the table, blinked at his cue and said:

"Not really. Air attack seems the only feasible possibility in this kind of limited war. There are all sorts of esoteric things, of course, like nerve gas, bugs, what have you—we've worried about them for years. But nobody's ever used them, nor will, except in the case of major world war, with no holds barred. The same way, a submarine in the Med. could drop an atomic warhead anywhere in the Middle East, but this is not going to happen because there'd be an immediate reaction from the other side. Aside from that kind of thing, I'd say that during the ceasefire matters have been organised so that no major or important attack by conventional means against the A.R.E.* heartland, and especially Cairo, would be able to succeed."

"By conventional means," Blackman repeated thoughtfully.

The brigadier looked worried. He had with him the information about the American STM17s and wondered again why he'd been asked to bring it.

"That's what I said," he replied levelly.

Blackman smiled, his manner conciliatory.

"I'm sorry if I seem to be talking in riddles. I'll try and take the matter a little further for you. There's time to fill in the background, because to be honest that's all I can do until our chap in Cairo gets one

*Arab Republic of Egypt—formerly United Arab Republic.

more but very important bit of confirmatory information. I don't think it'll be long arriving.

"Meanwhile it's the Foreign Office assessment that the ceasefire should weather the Tel Aviv killing, so far as the various governments themselves are concerned. Our job, as we see it, is to pour plenty of oil on the troubled waters, and the way to do this is to get organised a thumping great U.N. force, much bigger than the earlier ones, with comparable weapons to those of the Arabs and the Israelis, and the power to use them, if need be, in any circumstances. Whatever it takes, we want to see peace preserved in the Middle East. There are no qualifications to that policy. And, you can take it from me, that's straight from the top."

"D'you think the Russians would go along with that?" Grimwade asked.

"On the whole, yes. They're pretty sick of the regular crises and of having to feed more and more missiles and planes and advisers to the Arabs. If the Soviets could be sure they were getting somewhere with this, they'd no doubt feel differently, but all the evidence is that the Arab world is going to be just as divided, just as disorganised and just as fundamentally unsuccessful militarily as it has been for the last five years. On the other hand, while Israel feels insecure, she'll stay belligerent.

"Besides, the Russians have small respect for the Arabs and there's not much love lost in the other direction. No, the Russians would welcome an out, I feel. They'd much rather concentrate on South Asia, especially India and Ceylon, and if I were in their position I'd choose that way too, backing the Mesdames Gandhi and Bandaranaike.

"Come in . . ." he called, in response to a diffident knock on the door. A clerk brought in a single sheet of teleprinter flimsy and put it on the table before Blackman, who read it immediately.

"Well," he murmured. They all looked at him with greater interest, but for the time being he continued his previous line of thought.

"As I was saying, nobody wants a big war in the Middle East. It's too central, far too many other influential people would suffer. Southeast Asia, China—demonstrably it can be risked there, hence the Indo-China war, but the Middle East, no. A war of words, trade embargoes, nastiness on the borders, these things will go on, but the governments in Tel Aviv and Cairo, and their backers, don't want a real showdown."

"So is there a problem?" Stephen Roberts, one of the two academics on the committee, asked. An historian, he took a cynical view of the caution and pragmatism of his military and diplomatic associates.

"On the face of it, no," Blackman said slowly. "But although the governments and no doubt the peoples directly concerned don't want a war, it doesn't necessarily mean nobody does.

"Very relevant to this, unfortunately, is the disposition of several United States STMs."

"Whatever they might be," Roberts interposed with a show of irritability. "It's a wretched habit, this labelling of things with a set of initials, as though authority were afraid of their proper names. For Heaven's sake, old boy, don't call it a spade, call it an S.D.D."

"S.D.D.?" Blackman, who had a literal mind, was puzzled.

"Surface digging device."

Roberts had adroitly sugared his pill with humour. Everyone round the table grinned and the tension lessened, but Blackman had got the point.

"I tend to go along with you," he conceded. "And I apologise for using the initials, especially since you could have no way of knowing what they mean. As usual, in this case they are simply enough interpreted.

They mean 'small tactical missile'—although that isn't really specific becuase the thing isn't a missile at all but a bomb, and also becuase it doesn't let you know the STM is an atomic weapon. I'll not descirbe it to you—Brigadier Simons is the expert."

Simons spoke after a few moments of reflection.

"First off, over the last decade or so the really big atomic bombs, the fusion type, have proliferated so much on both sides they've pretty much cancelled themselves out. Everyone's scared stiff of them, soldiers perhaps most of all. These enormously powerful things are there, Heaven knows, in thousands, more than enough to kill all life several times over—and that's a considered estimate, not just a figure of speech.

"If they come into use it won't be war, as any professional understands it, just plain hell on earth. When it comes to using the big fusion weapons, you can count me in with the pacifists.

"What professional soldiers really wanted were field weapons, but evolving these hasn't been easy. You'll all know that even a low-power nuclear reactor is a very large object and atomic weapons of the fission type are really just reactors that've gone out of control. Mind you, there's no need to shield a bomb to prevent an extension of radiation, and most of the weight of a reactor is in the shielding.

"Even so, one of the major problems in developing field weapons has been to get them small and light enough to be readily handled. The world's first hydrogen bomb weighed fifty tons. Of course there's been the strongest kind of pressure to get this weight and size factor down, because of the requirements of submarine-launched missiles and to reduce the bore of atomic cannon.

"Other problems have come from the desirability of such bombs being 'clean.' There'd be little point in using any kind of weapon to get control of territory

13

—and that's what victory really amounts to—if it were going to stay radio-active for long periods of time. Hence there's been concentration on making weapons whose residual elements have a short 'half-life' during which their radiation can be dispersed to a safe level. This hasn't been altogether successful—we still haven't got rid of carbon 14. It has a half-life of eight thousand and seventy years."

Someone down the table coughed, and Blackman shifted uneasily in his chair.

"However, both sides now have quite a respectable array of field weapons," Simons continued. "Some are warheads for shells shot out of large, otherwise quite conventional guns, which are, however, not very mobile. A much simpler and more flexible technique is to have actual bombs, which one simply leaves behind, as one retreats, in a position the enemy is likely to pass through later. These can be exploded to order through the use of simple time fuses, or via radio links. The description of this type of weapons as STM was originally an American one, used in NATO communications."

"STM17?" Blackman prompted.

"What about security?" the brigadier asked.

"Surely we're all cleared here?" Roberts said impatiently.

"Indeed so," Blackman said soothingly. "However, as Brigadier Simons knows well, the essence of security is to tell nobody, no matter how well cleared, information they don't strictly need to know. In this case we don't need the classified details—it's more the size and power of the weapon that's significant to this meeting."

"I see. STM17 is one of the smallest of the American-manufactured atomic weapons. It's a fission-type device small enough to be carted round in a light truck and handled by a few men. It looks like a petrol drum, but somewhat longer and thinner. The troops call it the Bunger. The potential is so heavily classified I don't know it myself, but these things are made to have a limited and predictable explosive force, which is probably in this case a little below that of the Hiroshima bomb. That was the equivalent of twenty thousand tons of T.N.T."

"Limited!" Roberts commented, and pursed his lips.

"Very much so. The Russians are now said to be planning one hundred megation fusion warheads for their long-range missiles—the equivalent of one hundred million tons of T.N.T., or five thousand times the power of the Hiroshima bomb. SS9 I.C.B.M.s already in the Russian silos have warheads of twenty-five megatons."

There was general silence. Simons glanced inquiringly at Blackman, who said:

"That should do, thank you. I will add, however, that while the STM17 is a small weapon as such things go, it could virtually destroy a small city and would do considerable damage even to a large one. Also, 'clean' or otherwise, the radiation level is none the less destructive during and after the explosion."

He paused, and then added slowly, but without particular emphasis:

"There are four STM17s in an Israeli army store near the docks at Tel Aviv. I gather our government didn't know about this until after the weapons had actually been delivered, and then fought tooth and nail to have the Americans take them away again—however, without success.

"It all happened when the Israeli Prime Minister went to the United States back in October 1969, to ask Mr. Nixon for more weapons. So far as the public were told, these were specifically twenty-five Phantom jets and eighty A-4 Skyhawks. As you may know, Mrs. Meir was once a schoolteacher in Milwaukee, and she can speak with a persuasive voice, especially in the United States.

"She took a shrewd line, appearing not to question the Americans' insistence on controlling the Middle East power balance by providing only so many aircraft as they believed would not seriously disturb that balance. Mr. Nixon was gratified at this seemingly compliant reaction, and gave a hearing to Mrs. Meir's further contention that, within this situation of balance as assessed by the big powers, Israel still stood in grave danger in the event of a sudden all-out Arab military attack over the canal. In such a case, she wanted to have a major deterrent.

"Israel's only effective answer, she argued, could be field atomic weapons. There wasn't a need for many. She made the point that the Japanese surrendered after the dropping of the Nagasaki bomb because they believed the Americans had more atomic weapons. If, in the case of sudden Arab aggression, Israel could explode one, or possibly two, atomic weapons, this would probably deter the Arab advance for the same kind of reason.

"The Americans agreed, subject to an elaborate set of conditions. Israeli possession of the bombs was to be a secret, and it has indeed been a closely guarded one. The bombs were to be used only in combat, in consultation with the United States and only actually in Israeli territory. The use of the weapons in Sinai was specifically ruled out."

"So in general they seem safe enough," Roberts commented.

Blackman said nothing for the moment, but got up from his chair and stared through the window, which now revealed only darkness. Then he turned and spoke again, while remaining on his feet.

"I wonder if I can communicate to you something of what it must feel like to have access to these weapons, such convenient sources of decisive power if used in the right way? If you can, put yourselves inside the mind of a dedicated man, a trained soldier and sincere patriot, who must watch his country strike once, twice, three times, at its enemies—and win—yet never really see a prospect, even a hope, of final victory. The future remains one of a ceaseless war of attrition.

"This war drags on, not fought decisively in the field or in the air, but restrained by constant checks dictated by big-nation opinion and the world balance of power. At the same time comes blow after blow struck by terrorist organisations of the other side, who fight for the other side, but for which its governments refuse to take responsibility.

"Look back through the years—a school bus is bombed, half the children die and others are maimed for life, airliners are blown up in mid-air or hijacked, snipers pick off people working in their fields or travelling near the borders—and there's no sign of these things ending. Now comes the most insolent and grievous blow of all, the killing, in the centre of Tel Aviv, of the man who in himself was the rallying point of the struggle to survive in spite of Arab hostility.

"Mightn't the time come when even the most disciplined soldiers felt irregular action from the Israeli side might also be worth a try, especially if such an attack could so punish the enemy his will to fight was broken for good?"

"You're leading us to the thought," Grimwade said slowly, "that a sort of modern Stern Gang might commandeer one or more of these nuclear devices, get them into Egypt and explode them there, perhaps even in Cairo. I suppose it's possible, but surely there are too many good reasons why it's most unlikely . . ." he shook his head.

"But if they did, and succeeded," Blackman

persisted. "I want you to speculate as broadly as possible. Supposing by some accident American-made atomic weapons did explode in Egypt, or for that matter anywhere within the Communist spheres of influence. What would be the consequences?"

"Nuclear retaliation, in this case, against Israel," Brigadier Simons said at once. "Probably nuclear war throughout Europe, perhaps world war."

But Roberts took issue with him sharply.

"I can't agree, for the simple reason that all the powers involved know they would suffer themselves —terribly—from a nuclear war. What point could there be to it? Surely this is why nuclear weapons haven't been used in anger since Nagasaki?"

"But remember that in the case we are considering, atomic weapons would already have been used," Blackman pointed out. "What then? If you were a Russian leader, what would you do?"

"I still can't see that the other side could do much about it," Roberts insisted.

"Can't you? Put yourself in their position for a while. The bomb or bombs have exploded. There have been enormous casualties. A city has been destroyed. I agree that such matters could probably be tolerated, if necessary, within the power game of nations, all other things being equal. But all else would *not* be equal. Something else would now exist, a dangerous new precedent. Whatever the professed cause, American atomic weapons would have been used to the massive detriment of a Russian protégé. Soviet citizens, important ones, like military advisers and technical experts, would die.

"If the Communists let such a thing pass the first time, what would they do the next time, and the time after that? Think of the loss of prestige in global terms. Would they gradually allow themselves to be forced back against a wall? Again, could they really be sure the attack was not secretly sponsored by the

Israeli Government, perhaps even by the United States itself?

"Gentlemen, I have served in our embassy in Moscow and I am certain that is the way their line of thought would run. They would feel they could not allow such a situation to develop without insisting on some kind of retaliation—I hesitate to use the word revenge. This need not mean full-scale war—but something would happen somewhere. Whatever it might be, and where, we should much rather not find out."

For a full minute nobody spoke. Then Grimwade said:

"It's a persuasive line of argument in a way, but then, David, you're a persuasive type of man. With respect, a professional persuader. What about my earlier point? Surely this hideous idea, fortunately, just isn't likely. After all, the whole 'balance of terror' situation with atomic weapons is hedged around with problems too big for anyone to solve fundamentally. Why is this suddenly so important now? You've got a nigger in the woodpile somewhere, haven't you? Drag him out and let's see how black he is." He was not smiling.

Blackman took up the cable flimsy still lying before him on the table and leaned forward, a new urgency in his manner.

"The organisation of Israeli military men I postulated actually exists. We've known this for five weeks—also the identity of its leader and the fact that other influential people support him. They're mostly soldiers, but there are some politicians in it as well.

"During the last elections, the largest gain made by any group was that of the Gahal bloc, a right wing coalition that won 27 of the 120 seats in the Israeli Parliament, the Knesset. Gahal largely represents hard-headed businessmen, who want to see the war ended, decisively and for good. Israel is a small country in population and resources and even though her people work hard and make all kinds of sacrifices, although well-wishers in other parts of the world make money contributions, there could be only one end to a long-extended, indefinite war. Israel would be crippled financially in the finish. The Arabs would win by default.

"Naturally it's not the official policy of the Gahal parties, hawks though they may be, to support irregular operations against Egypt. However, we are sure that at least two of their members in the Knesset are in with the conspirators we're discussing, who show all the signs of being a very tough group indeed. We know them only by the name 'Jacob,' but that could as easily be the code name of the operation they're planning—for they're up to something, that we also know."

"How?" Roberts asked.

Blackman hesitated momentarily before replying:

"Colonel Rudzol, the man who runs this group, has a serviced flat in one of the new three-storied blocks in Arlosoroff Street in the Tel Aviv suburb of Zafon. A woman who cleans the apartments is our contact. Our man is often visited by his friends and at times they've been slightly careless because the old lady seems so stupid. However, she has an excellent memory. We asked her to tell us everything she heard, even seemingly meaningless snatches of conversation. It's surprising how often this method works, and how one can over a period build up a framework of facts. Soon there was no possible doubt to us that Rudzol and his associates were planning an independent action against the Arabs, although we had no clue as to what it might be.

"Then came an extraordinary chain of events. Our informant reported to us a name she'd heard. Naturally, we're always interested in names so we can enlarge our picture of the Jacob organisation. She thought it was Abu or Abdul Sharaf, but this had no particular significance, even after inquiries, to our people in Tel Aviv. As a matter of routine we circulated the information to all our posts in the Arab world and, sure enough, Cairo knew about a playboy academic named Abu Sharaf.

"He has an English girl-friend, and by a sheer stroke of luck our military attaché, while at a party, overheard this girl claim that Sharaf was really a Jew. It was a gay party, at which people say all kinds of stupid things, so nobody took any notice of her—except for our man, who already knew enough to be interested in Sharaf. We knew Sharaf was fond of boating on the Mediterranean, which is a strenuous sport to indulge in from Cairo, involving a long drive to and from Port Said, where he keeps this boat—the *Miranda*, she's called, a seventy-foot luxury cruiser, remarkably fast. Why Port Said, you may well ask, and not the yacht club at Alex? Port Said is, of course, a hundred and fifty miles or so closer to Tel Aviv.

"The girl-friend had problems we were in a position to help with, and so she agreed to talk. That was only tonight, and the results are in this cable. There is a radio transceiver in the *Miranda*, on which she several times overheard Sharaf speaking late at night, she claims, in Yiddish. That was what first put the idea in her mind that he could be an Israeli. Then of course other things came along that strengthened her conviction. Our informant doesn't speak or understand Yiddish, and taken by itself her claim might have been interesting, but too vague to pin much on.

"Then, as an afterthought, and without any prompting, she came out with a name she'd overheard Sharaf use several times in the course of a radio conversation and which she thought was the name of the person on the other end. It was Jacob."

He lapsed into silence.

"The bombs are guarded, of course?" Grimwade said at last. "These Jacob people couldn't get at them easily, surely? I've no doubt they're very well looked after."

Blackman's face formed a wry smile.

"Indeed they are. The STMs are guarded night and day, on a roster basis, by a crack army unit, a special duties commando group about whose loyalty there could be no doubt. It is an old-style elite corps of hand-picked men grouped around a leader who is himself something of a national hero."

"Colonel Rudzol?" Brigadier Simons inquired drily.

"Unfortunately, yes."

Two

"It's very late," James Clayshot, the British Prime Minister, said with a touch of asperity, then returned his attention to the paper Blackman had given him, summarising the views of the Middle East advisory committee.

"This is like a bad dream," he said a few minutes later, "and the argument's full of holes anyway. We can't prove a thing, can we?"

"No."

"In fact, I can't see we really know much more than we have done for some weeks. We've known about the bombs, and right from the start I regarded that as being risky. There's nothing new about the Jacob group, except for your Dr. Sharaf, with his boat. That is suggestive, of course."

"We thought you might want to warn the Israelis, perhaps unofficially. They could replace the guard unit, or just set people to watch Colonel Rudzol."

"Now look here," Clayshot said kindly. "I know how it is with you people. We've put you there to be watchdogs on a certain area. It's perfectly right and proper, only prudent, to keep an eye on various crisis spots so we can consider our involvement. It's just as correct for you to report to me as you've done. But action, however unofficial, on our part, is another matter. Once we act, we have to take the responsibility for whatever happens. Let's assume you're right about Rudzol and his people. Having them investigated might not help matters. They could go underground—worse still they might be forced into action they hadn't yet intended.

"Let's go through it again. This boat, the *Miranda* —where does she berth?"

"In the harbour at Port Said."

"So why do you think Cairo?"

"It's very much the obvious target."

"I suppose so. But it's what . . . a hundred and fifty miles up the Nile? Would he use his own boat?"

"Possibly, if that were absolutely necessary. He is trusted well enough to come and go as he pleases— certainly within A.R.E. territorial waters. Beyond that I think he'd need to smuggle the bombs through the delta by road or via the river and canals. There are thousands of *feluccas*, all pretty much alike, using the inland waterways. Once matters reached that stage—"

"I know . . . I know. But we still aren't sure, are we?"

"The bombs are there. We know the men guarding them are planning independent action. We know there's at least one man in Cairo, Sharaf, connected with this, that he's well-known and trusted, and that his boat can come and go freely, without arousing suspicion. So the opportunity and the machinery both exist. Now with the Defence Minister's assassination has also come a strong incentive."

Clayshot sighed.

"I follow your line of reasoning well enough," he said. "Also, I can see that possibly we could be kicking ourselves in a week, or a month, if we did nothing about it. It's the fact that we're involved only by virtue of our knowledge that sticks with me. We should be an outsider interfering, without much evidence to support our charges . . . an old woman hears a name, a common enough Arab name at that . . . a not very reliable younger woman, who doesn't speak Yiddish, thinks she recognises it. As for the radio and the fast boat, it could be just plain non-political crime, like smuggling, that Sharaf's up to.

"It's also important," he added, "that the very fact these weapons are in Israel is a red-hot secret. The last thing Tel Aviv wants is any boat-rocking about them."

Blackman thought about this for a few seconds.

"The bombs are American," he said. "A hint to Washington that there might be the slightest question about their safe-keeping . . ."

"That was also my thought. It's their business, or I should hope so. All very well, depositing those weapons over here. It's too close to us, too close to everything. They've got the Atlantic between them and the problem.

"Whatever else, you have convinced me enough to insist tomorrow, from my level, that the Americans make a security check. I'll ask them to use some pretext that will get the bombs out of circulation for the next week or so. That should be simple enough—they can plead a fault in the mechanism of that model and take them away for adaptation, something along those lines.

"Of course you'll realise their security people will be all over us like a rash? They'll want to know everything, including our sources of information. To keep you in practice, I'll refer them direct to you."

"Do you want me to tell them everything?"

Clayshot grinned.

"Not likely—no more than you have to, and even that needn't all be true."

It was midnight when Blackman got home, feeling tired almost to the point of numbness. Advancing age, he thought grimly, didn't make decision-taking any easier. Certainly one had more experience—knew more—but did that help? His wife, Barbara, was still up and she poured him a Scotch the way he liked it, without too much water. She watched him silently while he drank the first glass, then gave him another before saying:

"This came two hours ago, by special courier, on a motor-bike. It must be important."

Blackman opened the buff envelope and read the plain text decoding of the message from the British Embassy in Cairo:

SHARAF AND TWO OTHERS DROVE PORT SAID THIS AFTERNOON MIRANDA PUT TO SEA EIGHTEEN HUNDRED HOURS.

For some minutes he wondered whether he ought to ring Clayshot at once. He would no doubt be in bed and wouldn't welcome being roused—that special number was one to be used with discretion. Besides, was it so significant really? Sharaf took the *Miranda* to sea almost every weekend—what could be so different about this one?

For ten seconds he absently regarded the oily pattern of his drink as he swirled it methodically round and round the glass, then his gaze travelled slowly around the familiar living-room of his house, a little shabby but comfortable, and very reassuring. Photographs of their children, now grown-up with infants of their own, stood on the window-sill. The gramophone was playing the Rosenkavelier waltzes quietly in the background. Paddy, Barbara's Siamese cat, was stretched out on a shaggy mat before the electric fire.

Probably, he thought, he was over-tired, too anticipatory, seeing demons out of the corners of his eyes. Such was the rationalisation with which he went to bed. Yet sleep came only slowly, and even after it did, his dreams continued to be tinged with an uneasiness for which there seemed no obvious reason.

Late in the morning of the next day, Saturday, a message came from Tel Aviv reporting that the STM17s had disappeared from the army store at the docks.

Clayshot had been as good as his word. When he woke at eight o'clock he had spoken by radiophone to the ambassador in Washington. Immediate action was then required of the American Embassy in Tel Aviv. The United States ambassador there had swept aside an indignant Israeli reaction to his request that he personally sight the weapons and identify them, for such were his instructions. Accompanied by three of his own military experts, a C.I.A. man, several senior Israeli officers and the British military attaché, they arrived at the warehouse at ten-forty-five to find it deserted.

The crated STM17s were no longer inside. Hurried telephone calls revealed that Colonel Rudzol was away from his home, and that his whereabouts could not be established. This was also the case with the eighteen men who had been rostered on for the two shifts of the guard from five o'clock Friday evening until noon on that Saturday.

Amid the general confusion of high-level conferences it was a humble police inspector who discovered that the night watchman for the neighbouring warehouse had been one of several people who actually saw the bombs leaving. He had not long arrived on duty, at five-thirty the previous evening, when he saw the soldiers moving four large cases onto a military truck that had been backed into a loading bay. This had then moved off towards the wharves.

There, two old men who spent much of their spare time fishing saw the cases taken off and loaded with a portable sheerlegs, block and tackle, into a fast military launch. She had cast off not long after six and moved quickly out to sea, her twin Thornycrofts at full revolutions and her squat, broad stern well tucked down. The old men had watched her vanish into the dusk.

As soon as these facts became known an air and sea search of the Mediterranean coast as far west as the Marietta mouth of the Nile was commenced, but without much hope of success. Almost eighteen hours had passed since the bombs had left Tel Aviv, and it was probable that by now they would have reached their destination, or would be safely concealed in an interim one.

This was confirmed after the discovery about two o'clock by a search helicopter of the launch adrift and empty. It was boarded, towed back to Tel Aviv and carefully searched. The spacious forward cockpit, designed primarily for troop transport, was scratched and dented around its coamings. These marks were consistent with heavy weights having been loaded and unloaded hastily and without much care. The *Miranda* was not seen. She never returned to her moorings in Port Said. Sharaf disappeared. Rudzol and his eighteen men never went back to Israel.

The Israeli, British, and United States governments conferred urgently and heatedly. Israel was much blamed for a want of proper security, although there had seemed every reason to trust Rudzol. A war hero, a career soldier, a man outspokenly loyal to his country and to the assassinated Defence Minister, Rudzol had been chosen for the task of guarding the STM17s for these very qualities. It was only later that more disquieting facts were revealed. His wife had been forced to leave him because of his overbearing aggressiveness and irrational behaviour in private, which were in suspicious contrast to the icy calm and logic in action for which his army colleagues so much admired him. Indeed it proved that for nearly a year he had been under psychiatric treatment for a "limited disturbance," with both paranoiac and schizoid symptoms which, however, he had seldom betrayed in public.

The immediate point to be decided was whether or not the government of the Arab Republic of Egypt should be warned. The British ambassador then revealed all that was suspected about the Jacob organisation, and by five past four, only three minutes after he had stopped speaking, it had been decided that Cairo should be notified, so the Egyptian army and police could at least begin a search for the bombs before they could be moved inland. The cases containing the weapons were large and heavy, and distinctive in certain respects. This gave some hope that they might be traced, if the matter could be publicised thoroughly and quickly enough.

It was still assumed, for want of any real information, that the bombs were somewhere in the lower Nile delta, but this was not the case. After they arrived on the Egyptian coast in the *Miranda* they were transferred again to trucks and driven to Cairo at once. Rudzol and his men were experts, and knew that once the loss of the weapons was discovered, their freedom of movement must rapidly become limited. Hence it was important to act as swiftly as possible.

The joint warning was in the process of delivery to such bewildered Egyptian officials as could be found on a Saturday when, at 5.10 p.m., the first bomb exploded in Cairo.

Total damage extended for more than a mile in all directions from the explosion centre near Opera Square. Business houses, shops, restaurants, apartments, and hotels in that vicinity, including the

Continental-Savoy, were vaporised. It was later revealed that a Russian trade delegation, made up of seventeen senior officials, had been staying at the Continental-Savoy at the time.

The explosion, coming as it did towards nightfall, resulted in tremendous confusion, which the police could do little to control. All the roads soon became jammed with cars, bicycles, carts, animals, military traffic, and people on foot. Hundreds of thousands struggled to get out of the city, through which deadly radiation was already filtering. The size of the explosion, its characteristic firecloud and consequent pall of dust, through which columns of smoke soon began to push up, left few people in doubt as to its nature. Rumours spread quickly that world war had begun and that further atomic attacks could be expected.

These appeared to be confirmed when an hour after darkness there was a second explosion in the large modern suburb of Heliopolis on the north-east road to the airport, which was at that time congested by a tangle of traffic that had long since stopped moving. Sixteen minutes later came a third enormous explosion in the Arab city, centred near the revered university mosque of Al Azhar, which was accordingly blown into a fine dust after existing for not quite one thousand and three years. The population density in this area, together with its concentration of important historic and religious buildings, made this last explosion the most damaging of all. The fourth bomb was never used. Perhaps it had been dropped overboard during transshipment from the military launch to the *Miranda*, or its mechanism had been damaged by rough handling. There could be no way of knowing.

No accurate count of the deaths was ever possible, but calculations a year later indicated that of Cairo's population of four millions, probably just under a million and a half died because of the explosions, radiation sickness, and crushing and trampling of so many people during that dreadful night.

Radiation soon permeated relatively undamaged areas of southern Cairo and the surrounding countryside. The region of the capital was evacuated entirely, those who escaped being housed in makeshift camps throughout the delta. Ministers and officials who survived made their way to Alexandria, where a provisional government was established.

Three

*Memorandum to the Secretary
of State from the President*

The White House,
Washington.
November 12

MIDDLE EAST POSITION

I should appreciate it if you would prepare at once a paper covering the implications of the position, summarising the discussions we had at breakfast, stating areas of possible action by the Soviets, and listing any points made by members of the White House and State staffs that seem to you of major importance.

I communicated through the special teleprinter circuit with Mr. Brezhnev, suggesting to him, as we discussed this morning:

(i) that there should be a massive international aid programme on a crash basis to help the Egyptian refugees, and to restore Cairo as soon as radiation diminishes enough for teams to be sent in.

(ii) that special efforts be mounted, via frank and free discussions between the governments of the Soviets, the People's Republic of China, and ourselves, to avoid possible escalation.

Mr. Brezhnev declines to be committed on either main point. It is not going too far to describe his attitude as evasive. We have had no reaction yet from Peking.

In view of this, you should circulate your memorandum urgently, together with copies of this one, to senior officers listed in the National Military Command Authorities, so they may fill themselves in before we meet in the War Room at 2 p.m.

Meanwhile, for your information, I have ordered our defense potential and nuclear strike forces to full alert. While there is at present no reason to suppose any risk of this country becoming involved in war, the position is uncertain and all precautions are necessary.

Extract from a transcript of Radio Peking news broadcast on the foreign transmissions in English, November 12:

While the U.S. imperialists have tried with every possible kind of lie and evasion to shuffle off responsibility for the wiping out of Cairo, where it is now reported three-quarters of the people have died after three U.S. atom bombs exploded there, a tremendous wave of fury and indignation is sweeping the great Chinese people, who hold out the hand of pity and sympathy to our friends and allies in the Arab world, who have been so wickedly and wantonly attacked.

Meanwhile it is reported that steps have been taken to show the world the principle of Marxist-Leninist solidarity as interpreted by Mao Tse-tung through the setting aside of discussions on frontier and ideological points with the Soviet government, so the great peoples' governments may unite in the cause of world peace against the U.S. aggressors and their lackeys.

The provisional A.R.E. Government reports that

the Egyptian people accepts with gratitude offers of help from the Soviet peoples, and this assistance is already being provided through a huge airlift. In China's Fukien Province, children at a kindergarten near Foochow today resolved to work for two hours every evening growing beans to make money for the distressed children of Cairo.

The Alexandria Government has rejected angrily the suggestion that imperialist military personnel should enter Egypt under the pretext of helping victims of the disaster, for which the free peoples of the world have already tried and found the imperialists guilty. The A.R.E. has asked the Soviets, the People's Republic of China, and other friendly nations for active assistance, if necessary, to throw back such an invasion, and Soviet naval units in Port Said and Alexandria and off the Nile are already in a state of first readiness.

Meanwhile almost three-quarters of a million people have assembled in Tien An Men Square for a mass rally of protest and indignation against this terrifying consequence of U.S. imperialism. The scorpion must be crushed at once, even though it may bite back at the hands that bring it to account! The great Chinese people are ready and willing, if need be, to strain every muscle, break every sinew, in an effort for world peace . . .

Blackman tossed this paper, one of many flowing into the room at Downing Street, on to the green baize conference table. It was almost four o'clock, at which time he was due to have finished an assessment of world reaction which a Cabinet meeting was to use as a basis for discussion and action.

The door opened, and Blackman looked up. It was Clayshot. Typically, he wasted no time on greetings, but pitched straight into what he had to say.

"I looked in to tell you how glad I was you came to me on Friday—also I'm relieved I decided to act quickly on what you said. It wasn't at all our fault we were too late. Those bombs were already on their way out of Israel about the time we were last talking.

"Damned efficient, the military mind," Clayshot continued. "Prime it with any sort of crazy, half-baked idea, give it a hint of the direction of action expected, and it will proceed with the utmost expedition and self-discipline just as far as it can go, no matter how destructive and hideous the actual events turn out. You've only got to read service manuals on nuclear warfare to make that plain, and now the good soldier Rudzol has demonstrated the principle admirably.

"That's one good reason why politicians are necessary, Blackman—and diplomats. We know that no matter how bleak things look it's worthwhile going on talking—just talking. While people are still talking they're not killing."

Blackman knew Clayshot had this trick of speaking in abstract terms, but that his mind actually dwelt on concrete things, facts, possible action.

"So far as Britain's concerned," he responded. "That's our only hope."

"I'm glad you have that point well in mind. I have no doubt the Russians and the Americans are already fuelling their I.C.B.M. rockets, the anti-ballistic missile radars are already scanning, the atomic submarines are already on their way to their stations. If the missiles start flying, there'll no doubt continue to be small, primitive American, Russian, Chinese, Australian, and New Zealand societies—but I'm prepared to stake there won't be a Europe. There won't be much left here, Blackman!

"That's my main worry, on behalf of the people of this country. If it comes to world war, then we're finished, and you can be damned sure the planning generals everywhere are taking into account just that thing. On their equations, we can be cancelled out in advance. So when one puts all the talk and nonsense aside, there's only one possible line of action for me, isn't there? I could mobilise everyone, put the forces on full alert, but where would that get us?"

He sat down opposite Blackman and went on speaking slowly, thinking aloud.

"I read a military intelligence abstract a year or so ago that I thought to be basically important. It was a try at assessing the damage to this nation in the event of our joining in full-scale war as an ally of the United States. It was mostly guessing, naturally, but informed guessing on someone's part."

"How long did he give us?" Blackman asked quietly.

"The thing was based on our being attacked by nuclear submarines carrying Poseidon-type missiles, which they fired from stations in the Atlantic. Three submarines were postulated, each carrying sixteen SS6 warheads, which would be delivered almost simultaneously to give as punishing a first strike as possible. So it would be only a matter of hours, perhaps even minutes."

"And the consequences?"

"Guesswork again, of course. One-fifth of the population alive on the second day of the war, approximately eighty per cent of these survivors ultimately to die from radiation sickness. All the major cities destroyed. Six to ten per cent of our armed forces, other than ships at sea, still effective. Our missile subs could perhaps attempt a retaliatory swipe at Moscow, but I can't for the life of me disagree with Bertrand Russell's assessment that that would be morally dreadful. One would have to be pretty sick to get much fun out of 'sweet thoughts of a useless revenge', as the old boy put it.

"Anyway, those estimates of casualties were minimal figures. The Russians have well over a hundred submarines capable of firing missiles up to seven hundred miles, and these would be most adequate in our case. So a slightly greater concentration of missiles wouldn't be too difficult to organise—then everything and everyone'd be destroyed."

"Not much in it for us, is there?"

Clayshot shook his head. His face was grave.

"Somehow the peace has got to be kept. It isn't going to be easy. The president has got nowhere with the Russians. Brezhnev won't commit himself to anything, and why? Because they've something up their sleeves, I'll be bound, although what the devil it is I can't imagine." He paused, "Anyway, you'd better fill me in on the main facts from this mass of paper."

"I was just going to dictate the resume for the Cabinet meeting—"

"Then do it now, just rattle it off as if you were reporting to me verbally. That'll keep it simple and informal. Miss," he told the stenographer at the other end of the table. "Just you take this down the way Sir David says it—my questions too—and type it out afterwards as quickly as you can.

"Now, first—is there anything that seems out of character about Russian or American activity? I don't mean routine military preparations, but the sort of thing that might shed some light on the future."

Blackman thought about this.

"There's nothing I've seen I'd call really unusual, that I wouldn't have predicted. Probably the closest thing to what I think you mean has been the very rapid Russian takeover of the government of the A.R.E. Early reports indicate that Russian control of the country was almost immediate, as though there might have been a prearranged plan. Our nationals, and the Americans, are already in trouble. The consuls in Port Said and Alex, their expatriate staff, plus all other people of Western citizenship were rounded up this morning and given only an hour to get out on special aircraft. Anyone still there is liable to immediate arrest and internment. Perhaps that's as well, for their own protection. Heaven knows what an Egyptian mob might do to them once the full significance of the Cairo explosions dawns on them."

The faces of both men were grim.

"It's very bloody and shows all the signs of becoming more so, doesn't it?" Clayshot said. "What about Tel Aviv? I know already, by the way, that they're calling on the United States to stand by them in the event of a direct attack on Israel. The Prime Minister has refused to leave the country at such a critical time. Instead he's sent off that ex-airforce chap of theirs—the one who spells his name differently from his father . . ."

"The Transport Minister?"

"That's the one. Anyway, he's bound for Washington to rally support there in the event of big trouble. I should imagine the President'd be mighty cautious about that. Nothing's been said publicly of course, but for the record the Israelis are calling on the U.N., the Soviets, and the United States to guarantee the neutrality of the whole Middle East region. Now, do you have anything more?"

"Just before you came in, Tel Aviv reported they were expecting a similar appeal from the Israelis to us."

"Are they indeed? Well, we can kill that one before it even hatches.

"Now then, there are one or two things I want you to do for me. Hand over this job to someone else reliable, go home, get packed and stay there until my office gets in touch. If my plans work out we shall be flying to Moscow as soon as possible. We shall land in Paris and pick up Dubois, who can speak for the West European countries. Like us, they have no enthusiasm for being wiped out, and we're hoping a joint approach might succeed in prising out of the Russians what they want, what they intend to do. It's plainly hopeless for the Americans to try and negotiate further at the moment, yet nothing could be more dangerous than a total breakdown in communications. Then the military mind would take over, God help us all.

"Whatever the Americans might think or feel, there's going to have to be a pound of flesh in this somewhere. The Russians will want a reckoning, and it won't be a trifle, to balance up the account. You've always believed that, haven't you? I recall coming across the thought several times in the minutes of your meetings."

Blackman nodded.

"Now more than ever. While I was serving in Moscow the Sino-Soviet ideological dispute was at its height, and it was made very plain then that Russian political action is practically mechanised. Every little polemical, geographic, or historic point about the banks of the Amur River was painstakingly answered. If there was a comeback from the Chinese, then there'd be another answer. If a ball is played to the Russians, then it will be hit back. It's as simple as that. They let *nothing* pass."

"I see. Of course, that's why the president's got no change out of Brezhnev. Now it's my opinion that if anyone's going to have to suffer over this, it'd better be the Israelis. I know the whole ghastly business has been a mistake but that doesn't remove the consequences. The bombs were theirs, Rudzol was their man, and no matter how often and energetically they argue he was a freelance, there must remain the lurking suspicion that he wasn't. Certainly now," he added gloomily, "the poor bloody Arabs don't want to fight anyone.

"So you might turn that over in your mind and

think about what we could suggest as a starter if the Russians agree to meet us, but don't seem to have definite ideas of their own. Next, let's organise some public relations work. Get Hewitt in Tel Aviv to push the Israeli Government around a little. Have him tell them they'll get no help from us if it comes to war. Tell them that, in the convenient phrase of the Japanese, they'd better adopt a low posture. The more fuss they can make about blackguarding Rudzol and putting up a hunt for him and his gang, the better. You can tell them that goes for the Nine in Europe as well.

"I must get away now, but listen to the B.B.C. news at seven. Whatever we decide in Cabinet will be released then, and it's as quick a way as any of your getting to know about it. Speaking of the B.B.C. gives me an idea—ask them to get their man in Tel Aviv to drum up a story—a think piece if need be—about the hunt for Rudzol, then run it for all they're worth on the foreign services."

Blackman sent an urgent coded cable to the Embassy in Tel Aviv, then rang up the B.B.C. newsroom.

"We don't much like making up stories," the duty chief of staff said doubtfully.

"Take it from me, it's important—couldn't be more so. Do you want me to ring up Lord—"

"Oh, no, that's not necessary," the B.B.C. man broke in impatiently. "Leave it to me. I'll wire them right away."

"Besides," Blackman added, "it'll turn out to be authentic. We know the Israelis are going to take that line. They're scared stiff."

"So should I be. All right. We should have it on at seven."

"As soon as that?"

"Why not? It doesn't take long to write that kind of story off the top of one's head."

Blackman laughed.

"Thanks anyway."

"Should I move my family out of London? We have a place in Scotland," the voice on the other end of the wire asked, in different tones. "Do you people really know?"

"Not really. Not yet."

"Is your family still in London?"

"Yes, they are."

Blackman thought this conversation over as he drove home. The traffic was a shade heavier, he imagined, but there was no indication of panic, not even a minor sign of crisis. The people in their cars, walking, or climbing aboard buses seemed exactly the same as usual. There was no telling what was going on inside their minds, but there must be quite a few who were wondering if it wasn't time to run for cover.

Scotland? It would need to be a good deal farther than that, to be safe. He looked around the peaceful, orderly streets and tried to visualise what it must have been like in Cairo. If the Israelis could locate Rudzol, make a public example of him, at least that might take some of the sting out of the situation.

At home Barbara was listening to the radio.

"You're early," she said. "I didn't expect you till all hours. What's the matter?"

"Nothing really. Nothing new, anyway. But the P.M.'s expecting to make a journey, and he says he'll want me along."

"Where to? Bermuda?"

Blackman laughed.

"Just because he's a Labour man you don't have to be that cynical about him. Actually he's taking a very shrewd, realistic attitude towards this business, from

41

Britain's point of view. We aren't going to be full of glory, but also dead, if he can help it.

"And much as I'd like a few days in Bermuda the plans are for a much cooler climate, just between you and me, Moscow."

Barbara pursed her lips.

"Moscow, eh? A nasty dangerous place at the moment."

"Possibly. They might not have us, of course."

Barbara went upstairs to pack a bag for him, leaving him alone with the first of his two usual Scotches and water. He was at a loose end, with nothing definite to do after so many hectic hours, and wandered about the room, picking up a magazine for a few minutes, then throwing it down again without really taking in anything on its pages. So he killed time until Barbara came back to have the second drink with him. It was then a few minutes before seven and he went over to the radio, turning the volume higher for the news.

"A Cabinet meeting has just ended, and the Prime Minister has made a statement of Britain's attitude in the present world situation. Russian and Chinese sources claim that well over a million people died in Cairo, but added that radio-activity in the city is now subsiding. The Communist powers have made bitter attacks on the United States and Israel and have placed their armed forces on full alert. The Israeli Government is making a full-scale search for the missing army officer and his associates whose secret conspiracy resulted in the Cairo tragedy.

"The Prime Minister, Mr. Clayshot, said tonight that after urgent consultations with defence and foreign office specialists, the Cabinet had decided on a policy of unequivocal British neutrality in the event of hostilites arising from the present world situation. He added that similar statements were expected from the governments of France, West Germany, and other

European nations with whom Britain had been consulting.

"Mr. Clayshot said: 'There is no thought in our minds of disloyalty, unfriendliness, or failure to honour the spirit or letter of our treaty obligations. Our initiative comes from the feeling that it is the duty of every nation at this time to declare itself plainly for peace.

" 'Due to a tragic accident nuclear weapons have been used and as many as a million people have already suffered. Should war result we are unhappily certain it would be a nuclear war, and this could, indeed probably would, end life as we know it in Britain and perhaps also in Europe. Hence it seems to us that we should at once make clear our position to the super-powers so there can be no doubts about what it is. Britain will remain neutral, no matter what happens, unless we are ourselves attacked. I can see no advantage in alerting the armed forces. My advice to everyone is to go quietly about their affairs.'

"First reaction from Washington is that the United States understands and respects the British view. So far, there has been no comment from Moscow."

"A bold move," Barbara said.

"I agree. Not everyone would have done it, so promptly, without shilly-shallying."

The bulletin was not long over when the 'phone rang.

"For you," Barbara said.

It was Roberts, Clayshot's private secretary.

"We shan't be doing any flying tonight," he said.

"It was no, then?"

"I fear so. Mind you, the matter's still under consideration in Moscow. We got the impression the door hadn't been quite slammed, and the old man has told our people to keep a foot in the crack as long as possible. We've done all we can—now it's up to the Russians."

43

Four

In Moscow Commodore Baitak looked out on to the square below, a picture fast blurring in the dwindling light. Snow patterns grew on the lower part of the windowpanes as the temperature went on falling. These frost pictures on the glass reminded him of his youth far off in the east where, in a small town on Lake Baikal, his father had been a judge. It had been a difficult background for Baitak to live down, possible only through the exercise of diligent correctness.

He was glad it was now almost time to go home. His files were complete, his table neat and arranged, as he always liked his affairs to be at this time of late afternoon. Whatever paper came his way he took pride to answer the same day. This principle had served him well during a long but undistinguished administrative career in the Soviet Navy. It was said that Baitak was sound. To be sound was good, better indeed than to be brave if that also meant being too original.

His reverie snapped back to the present, the real picture through the window of heavily coated pedestrians plodding through the deepening snow, of cars whose back wheels spun on icy roads. Yet tonight the picture was not the same as usual. No streetlights were on, blinds had to be drawn to maintain Moscow's blackout, and cars, trucks and buses crept forward along the thin slits of light escaping from headlamp masks issued only that day.

The telephone bell jangled. Baitak looked at the wall clock opposite his desk. It was three minutes from the time the day's work officially ended, ten minutes from that at which an officer of his seniority might decently leave. In the foyer beyond the open door of his office his secretary had already packed away her knitting in a capacious handbag and clipped plastic goloshes over her shoes. So, he must now take the call himself.

At this hour, he thought, it would probably be his wife Stefanie asking him to buy something at the Metro shops on his way home. But when he answered he found it was not Stefanie.

"Yes, comrade," he snapped. Why, he thought, should Komorov ring, and at such a time? And his meaning was at first far from clear.

"A terrible line, Comrade Admiral," he interposed. "Please repeat . . . yes, again if you don't mind. Zagrev? Paul Zagrev, Captain, why yes, I know him, of course . . ."

He nodded slowly as Komorov's asperic words filtered, Lilliputian, through the earpiece. Then there was silence, a solid silence he could not at first find words to penetrate.

"Hullo, hullo," Komorov said impatiently. "Are you there Baitak . . . damn it, has this blessed line gone again?"

"No, I'm still here, comrade. You were speaking of Zagrev?"

"You know where he is?"

"After he was detached from seagoing service he was sent to me for employment. He's working in the requisitions office of C destroyer branch. Of course he'd be going home now . . . No, I don't know . . . *who* wants him? Comrade Grechko . . . which Grechko? Comrade Marshal, the minister? Why yes, at once . . . at once."

"Now listen carefully, Baitak. I don't know this
45

Zagrev myself, only that memo of his that stirred up such a fuss and bother. Now someone higher up, maybe even the Defence Minister himself, must have got hold of a copy. They're interested. That's why the marshal wants to talk to Zagrev. Do you know what this famous memo's about?"

"No."

"It came through my office, of course, with all the other paper from the strategic studies school. I haven't got time to read everything that goes across my table . . . who has? . . . but I do know Zagrev's submission caused trouble politically. It was felt an officer of his rank had no right to address his superiors on matters of nuclear strategy. He isn't even a party member . . . anyway, that's the background to why he was sent to you for a desk job."

"I understood that he was in disgrace," Baitak said.

"Yes, but anyone can make a mistake. Zagrev had an examplary record before that. Well-educated—he was a diplomat before the war, did you know that? . . . the submarine service during the war, steady progress after that to second in command of a nuclear boat—no question about his loyalty. Where Zagrev is concerned I feel the picture is changing."

"Yes, comrade."

"Just as well for you to understand that. Now, get a car, go to the requisitions office of C destroyer branch, wherever that might be, and find out where Captain Zagrev is. Pick him up and when you've got him, ring me immediately on Central 25097. I'll be here, waiting for the call."

"It must be tonight?"

"Didn't I tell you it was Comrade Marshal Grechko who wanted him? Within two hours will do."

That was all. The receiver clicked as Komorov replaced the headset at the other end. Baitak cursed under his breath as he looked gloomily out into the square, where the snow was now heavier. It would probably take an hour for a car to make its way to the office, seven miles away, in which Zagrev worked. But, of course, Zagrev would not still be there, he recollected uneasily. Here, Baitak, he told himself sharply, use your brains! While he had never met the six foot tall, intimidating figure of the Defence Minister, his reputation was enough to inspire respect. Baitak understood that if he bungled this, his career and perhaps even more would be at stake.

So he took up the telephone again and asked the operator to put him through to the building in which the offices responsible for C destroyer branch supply were located. There was no answer from the duty officer's number, and one after another the extensions in the building rang monotonously, without any reply. Baitak's spirits fell, and his voice became harsher and more peremptory as the minutes passed. Eventually the telephonist raised the home number of a paymaster officer who lived nearby. Baitak sent him back to the office at once to get Zagrev's address from his records.

It was quite dark when the paymaster rang through with the information, and the address he gave would take at least forty minutes to reach. Just as Baitak was to leave, the phone rang again but he did not touch it, but went out leaving it still shrilling behind him.

Zagrev's home was in one of the large, featureless blocks of apartments built in the north-west of the city after the German war. Number 8 was on the ground floor, opening off the foyer. However, it was in darkness and there was no response to Baitak's repeated knocking at the door. He concluded there was nothing for it but to wait, and reflected ruefully on the pleasant meal awaiting him at home, his warm apartment, and carpet slippers. This line of thought reminded him that he had not phoned Stefanie, who by now would without doubt have worried herself into a migraine. He turned with the intention of finding a telephone when a tall, steady-eyed man whose greying temples belied a youthful appearance of face and figure came to the door of Number 8, taking out a key with difficulty, since under his left arm he carried a number of parcels.

"Comrade Zagrev?"

The man turned, and raised his eyes inquiringly.

"Yes."

"You take some finding. I may say!"

"I've only been out shopping for food," the other man said, good-humouredly. "What's your hurry?"

"I'm Baitak. We haven't met personally, but you'll know my name."

"Of course. I'm sorry you've been inconvenienced waiting for me—"

"Say nothing about that!" Baitak interposed, in better countenance now. "There's no way you could have known we wanted you."

"Wanted me?"

"Indeed. Urgently, most urgently. It's the Comrade Minister of Defence himself who wishes to see you. It's about that memorandum of yours—please don't mention further that I told you that, but you ought to be prepared."

To Baitak's amazement Zagrev merely nodded slowly, as if this were to be expected.

"You've read what I wrote, comrade?"

"No, I've not had that pleasure," Baitak returned courteously, recollecting that Zagrev might yet turn out to be an important man. "But we must keep a weather eye on the time"—he enjoyed using nautical terms, perhaps because he had always been a desk sailor—"A telephone? Good." And he went to the public booth in a dark corner of the foyer and dialled Central 25097.

"It's Baitak."

"Baitak? You have Zagrev?"

"I'm with him now, at his apartment."

"Excellent. Take him, will you, in your car straight to Comrade Marshal Grechko's *dasha* in Arkhangelskoye—this is the exact address—and report to the comrade minister with him. I've been advised he'll expect you at any time between seven-thirty and nine. It should be possible, if you leave now, to arrive, when . . . ?"

"By eight-thirty," Baitak replied.

"Very good. I'll advise the comrade marshal's aide."

"And what shall I do after that?"

"Just take your orders directly from the comrade marshal."

The car reached the *dasha*, set back in large, well-kept grounds by Moscow standards, at eight-twenty, and it was just on the half hour when they were ushered into a large, heavily panelled study. Pink light from ornate shades overhead seemed absurdly out of key with the gnarled, fox-like face of the big man behind the desk. Grechko did not rise or smile when they entered, merely asking:

"Which of you is Zagrev?"

The captain identified himself.

"And your companion? Does he have anything to do with your ideas?"

Baitak said: "No—it was just my duty to bring him to you, comrade."

"You've done so. Now you can go." And he turned his attention wholly to Zagrev, ignoring Baitak as he backed out the door, his ears stinging from his curt dismissal.

"Well now, Comrade Zagrev," Grechko said with more animation. "You'll take a glass of vodka, I'm sure."

He indicated the bottle beside him on the tray with

some glasses. Zagrev, who was a sparing drinker, filled a glass half-full and set it down beside him. Grechko's eyes followed his every movement.

"You've had a good reputation, Zagrev, through most of your career," Grechko said at last, placing his hand on a folder on the desk. "I have your file here. There's little in it to complain of. I see a few student pranks are listed, rather too broad contacts when you served in our embassy in Canberra, but nothing untoward."

Zagrev acknowledged this with a nod.

"Fault was found with you, however, over the memorandum concerning nuclear warfare you sent in. Why did you write that?"

Grechko's tone was mild, but Zagrev recognised the necessity now to summon all his limited powers of expression.

"Comrade Minister, when one works as I did for several years in nuclear submarines, with fusion missiles in the launchers, one is compelled to think more than ordinarily about the consequences that would follow their use. If, of course, we were attacked directly—say by the U.S. with atomic weapons, a return blow as massive as possible must be—logical."

"Logical?" Grechko mused. "An unusual word, perhaps, yet on the whole I agree with it. Whatever the hawks in the Pentagon might think, no sane man, even a wicked Russian, could actually relish the thought of killing millions, especially since it would also inevitably mean substantial losses of our own people. But go on."

Reassured by this comment Zagrev continued more confidently:

"But it seemed to me that if a crisis came, as it probably would, in circumstances less straightforward than direct nuclear attack, we could do well to have formulated beforehand a definite policy, which still remained a step short of total nuclear war, and therefore forced the final decision back on the other side."

Grechko nodded.

"Strange thinking for a naval captain—yet of course you were previously a diplomat."

"The Comrade Marshal may not know, but ideas were invited by the strategy school I'd just attended —we were ordered to think freely about the tactics of nuclear war."

"What you suggested was hardly a tactic."

"I expect not. Indeed, I was much criticised for it, I'm told. I think it was felt I'd gone beyond strategy into the political field, an area in which suggestion was presumptuous."

"As it was, you'd agree?"

"On reflection, yes. But my intentions—"

Grechko held up his hand, poured himself vodka, but did not offer more to Zagrev. He remained silent while he drank it, appearing to be immersed in deep thought.

"It is an interesting mystery," he said at last, "how the flow of human ideas works. Your paper came to my attention only because a clerk sent me in a wrong file. I opened the memorandum at page two, and began to read.

"Now I'll tell you something, for your own ears alone. This business in Cairo, according to our own information, probably happened just as the Americans and Israelis said it did. The story of the irregular group launching the attack on its own initiative, I repeat, is very likely to be true."

Zagrev sat silently, but his pulse began to rise.

"It was remarkable," Grechko went on. "Just how close a parallel this is with the case—purely hypothetical—you had written down on page two of your paper. This struck me at once, and I went on reading. I will not conceal that I am taking your proposals quite seriously. How long did you think about it all, before you drafted the memorandum?"

"The matter had been on my mind for many months, perhaps even years, Comrade Minister. I lay awake at night thinking about it. I didn't of course like what seemed the inescapable conclusion, on purely humane grounds. Yet I believed it would prevent much worse things, and I could not see any alternative, from our point of view."

"You'd agree it doesn't entirely eliminate the risk of war?"

"An element of such risk remains, yet I think that given the right circumstances, it would be a very slight one. We should need to launch the plan from a position of power, right on top of an earlier strong initiative. It should be the last of two, or even better, three unpleasant surprises we gave the enemy. Then, of course, much would depend on the choice of the place."

"You haven't put that strongly enough," Grechko retorted. "Everything depends ultimately on that. You've listed the factors. It must be a place that had already alienated much of world opinion, that is known to have followed aggressive policies—in other words, one of the more hawkish allies of the United States. It must be sufficiently isolated for any fallout not to affect more innocent neighbours. It should have dispersed defences, so the operation must be bound to succeed, and no retaliatory capacity within its own command.

"I will add one more requirement you couldn't possibly have foreseen: A coastal city roughly the same size as Cairo."

Grechko spun the illuminated globe—a pretty toy—that stood on his desk and laid a broad finger on it. Zagrev looked, and nodded.

"There isn't anywhere else that meets all the requirements, is there?" the minister asked.

Zagrev shook his head. A vague but terrible uneasiness stirred at the back of his mind, but he shook it off.

"Very well, thank you for your help, Captain Zagrev. Tell me, would you like to go back to sea again?"

"Yes, comrade."

"You don't like routine paper work much?"

"Not as a career."

"Well, I'll see what can be done. You'll be hearing from your superiors again soon, I think. Are you married, any family?"

"I was married, comrade, with one daughter," Zagrev said stolidly. "They both died in Leningrad, during the German war."

"Then you have no ties. That's as well. Thank you again, Captain. You may go now."

The next day Zagrev found himself ordered, at a few minutes' notice, to Admiral Komorov's office. He was ushered in without delay, an indication of the importance of the matter.

Komorov was not alone. Seated on a chair flanking his desk was a stocky man, probably in his late thirties, with liquid, resentful brown eyes and dressed in a naval uniform with which Zagrev was not familiar. He met Zagrev's glance without signs of interest or animation.

"Captain Zagrev?" Komorov greeted him coolly. "Please sit down. Will you meet Commander Said Gamal, a colleague from the navy of the A.R.E.? Commander Gamal has been here for some months, on secondment and high-level training in our submarine force. He will now proceed to sea in association with you, Captain Zagrev.

"You are ordered to proceed by air to Port Said and take up command of our nuclear submarine

Novgorod, which is now attached to the Mediterranean Fleet. Her movement to Port Said has been authorised, and you'll find her there when you arrive. *Novgorod* will be attached to the A.R.E. Navy, and Commander Gamal will act as the representative on board of the provisional government of the A.R.E.

"Regardless of this, authority for the discipline and actions of the ship will remain in your hands, Captain Zagrev, and *Novgorod* will stay within the normal chain of command of the Soviet Navy. Decisions as to her movements will be taken at the political level, in consultation with the provisional government of the A.R.E."

Komorov, who had been speaking slowly and formally, now relaxed.

"Well then," he went on. "That's as much as I can tell you for the moment. I'm glad you've met and wish you a useful association."

Zagrev forced himself to smile, although it was difficult enough in the circumstances, for Gamal had said nothing, and his face was still tensed in the same glassy stare. When Zagrev looked steadily and curiously at the Egyptian, he noticed a slight but regular tic in his left eye, a sure sign of strain brought on, he wondered, by what?

But this would never do! He felt he must awaken some response in Gamal even if it were a hostile one, so he rose to his feet, crossed to Gamal's chair, and held out his hand. Zagrev felt the other man's fingers grip his convulsively. Gamal's hand was burning as though he were running a high fever.

"You'll be on Flight 3/13 to Port Said today," Komorov said, watching the two men curiously. "It's due to depart at 1500 hours. Here are your travel documents . . . and your papers, Captain Zagrev, to take over *Novgorod*."

He rose, the other men did likewise, and he moved with them to the door.

"Good luck," he said, without emphasis, and shook hands. Zagrev stood aside to let the Egyptian pass first and Komorov then added:

"If you'll excuse me, Commander Gamal . . . there are some administrative matters I have yet to discuss with Captain Zagrev. I've no wish to delay you, so I'll say good-bye."

Gamal acknowledged this with a nod and walked away towards the lifts.

"Sit down again, Zagrev," Komorov said. "I wanted some words with you alone. You've been given, from the very highest level, command of *Novgorod* and her mission." His cool phrases indicated that these decisions had been made over his head and, perhaps, against his inclination. "That being so, it's important you fully understand your responsibilities. Do you know the *Kiev* class? Of course not. *Novgorod* is only the second of them, and she was commissioned just two months ago. She isn't so different from *Irkutsk,* your last boat, all the same."

He took up a small bound folder, opened it, and passed it across to Zagrev. It contained side and top elevations and cutaway perspectives of the elongated modified spindle hull typical of all high-speed nuclear-powered submarines, with annotations describing the accommodation, machinery compartments, armament, and associated equipment.

Zagrev looked it over carefully, but could find little that differed from the older *Irkutsk,* with which he was so necessarily familiar he could have found his way through any of her corridors and compartments in absolute darkness. The major respect in which the *Kiev* class seemed to differ was the larger size of the missile compartment aft of the conning tower. This compartment was even longer than the reactor and machinery rooms. Also, the conning tower was farther forward than usual, so the missiles were close to the balance point of the hull. Instead of the usual sixteen SS6 missiles, these newer boats had twelve larger ones. These, and their launching tubes, pointing upwards for firing while the boat was submerged, ran the full depth of the pressure hull from the keel to the upper cladding, which was in the form of a flat deck.

Otherwise the submarine seemed to have little offensive armament. Her torpedo tubes in the bow were of smaller diameter than was usual in a major submarine class, and there appeared to be only six, each armed with homing anti-submarine missiles. One light quick-firing gun was mounted in a special compartment, that could be sealed off while submerged, in the conning tower.

Komorov waited patiently while Zagrev studied the drawings, then smiled slightly as he raised his head.

"Our biggest and best," Komorov commented mildly.

"They're enormous missiles," Zagrev replied, "Almost I.C.B.M.s."

Komorov nodded.

"The *Kiev*-class submarines are specialised for them—they're Lenin missiles, our answer to the American Poseidon. The keel of the boat is specially strengthened to take the shock of firing these big rockets. Each one weighs eighteen tons. Also they have a greater range than anything of this sort we've built before—solid propellants give them an accurate 2,800 miles. They are MIRV vehicles, of course, each with three nuclear warheads. There are built-in electronic and metallic chaff defences against A.B.M.s, and control is by modified inertial guidance systems. Once dispatched, we believe there's nothing that can stop them."

Komorov's voice had gained enthusiasm, and his face was more animated and flushed, as he discussed *Novgorod*'s potential. He was obviously proud of her.

But Zagrev's hand shook slightly as he handed the manual back to Komorov, who methodically restored it to his drawer.

"When?" he asked.

"That hasn't been decided," Komorov said quickly. "Don't presume, Captain Zagrev, that matters will necessarily take the theoretical course you recommended. It is nevertheless true that your ideas have been considered seriously.

"The final decisions will be entirely political ones and may yet depend upon events. You will await your orders in Port Said. I don't think it will be long before they decide, one way or another. Now for the moment I think that's all . . ."

He gave a wintry smile and extended his hand again.

"One moment, Comrade Admiral—there is a point that worries me somewhat," Zagrev said.

"Then I'd better know what it is."

"It's Commander Gamal. I have to admit his manner troubles me a good deal. He is very much under stress. The expression of his face shows that, his eyes are almost those of a madman, and I noticed a steady, involuntary tic of an eye-muscle. These things are all signs of great inward strain, even instability. Is he the right man for such an important mission?"

"We haven't much choice," Komorov admitted. "He happened to be here with us, he has the necessary seniority, and he is a loyal friend of the Soviets.

"As for his manner, and the signs of strain, I believe you will find these understandable when I tell you that his father and mother, his wife and his three small sons, were all in Cairo last Saturday evening."

Five

Michael Rule had decided that afternoon to relax with a light novel in an easy chair in his Cairo flat, but the plot of the book was not all it might have been, and before long he had drifted off to sleep.

He was awakened by a searing flash of light that seemed to burn its way through his closed lids on to the eyeballs, even though he was facing away from the explosion centre. This impression was so marked it left an after-image, of jagged shape, superimposed on whatever he looked at for almost a minute afterwards.

The building was meanwhile hit by a shockwave so severe it felt like an earthquake. The big plate windows on the side facing the city blew in with such force that one of the shards of glass flew across the room to cut Rule's arm slightly. Startled, he looked towards the city centre, some six miles away. It was now clouded by a dense layer of dust that seemed to grow larger and more oppressive with each moment. Then several columns of dark smoke appeared from its top surface and surged upwards.

Rule then understood that this was an atomic explosion, and that he could not now go to the Embassy, as he had at first intended. He put on shoes, took his passport, money, and car keys from the bedroom, and went down to the garages.

When he turned the car from a sidestreet on to a main road leading to the open countryside of the delta, he had to wait some time to enter the stream of traffic. It was denser than usual, although not yet markedly so. During these moments of waiting, Rule, who was a bachelor without urgent personal responsibilities, decided that there was little point in staying in the vicinity of Cairo. He would be best out of Egypt altogether, and the sooner the better.

The British mission in Cairo had not been told about the missing bombs until minutes before the first explosion. Even then, only the ambassador himself had known. Rule thus had no reason to connect the disaster with Sharaf, and the events he had earlier investigated. Like most other people in the city, he assumed that atomic war had begun, probably on a world scale, and that the attack on Cairo was merely part of what must be happening everywhere.

Rule would probably have reached Alexandria and left the country before the attacks on and arrests of European and American nationals began, but for a trivial accident. The vehicle immediately ahead of his car stopped without warning. As soon as he heard the tyre-noise Rule kicked the brake pedal, which went to the floor without effect. New rubbers had been fitted to the master cylinder only days before, and Rule cursed the slovenly mechanic who had got a small speck of dirt into the hydraulic system. The next time he pumped the pedal the brakes worked.

Even so the car was still moving slowly when the top of the radiator shell hit the high tray of the truck in front. At once the engine stalled. When Rule pressed the starter button the solenoid clicked sharply, but the motor would not turn over. He tried several times again, with the same result, and before long the traffic began to diverge around him.

When he got out and raised the bonnet, he found the radiator had been pushed back so the fan blades were driven lightly into the soft metal of the core. A thin stream of water trickled from a split in the header tank.

Just then the sky was arced by another brilliant flash and there was a shockwave and a low rumble of sound as the Heliopolis bomb exploded. This time, perhaps because he was farther from the centre, Rule actually heard the explosion, although the sound was strangely muted. He noticed, too, that the stream of vehicles was denser, and moving more slowly. It now occupied the full width of the road, and there was no longer any eastbound traffic. Although the car appeared to be only slightly damaged, it was bad enough to make his chances of getting it moving again very slight. It was seven o'clock—ten hours yet to dawn.

Rule suspected that the slight breeze coming from the direction of Cairo must soon bring an invisible but dangerous mist of radiation. The wind could easily freshen, and then matters would rapidly become worse. His mind travelled back to the nauseating descriptions of radiation sickness he had read in service manuals, and these thoughts quickly brought a decision to abandon the car. He put on his coat and began to walk briskly along the verge of the road, which was brightly lit for a few feet beyond the bitumen by the hundreds of headlamps. Just then came the dull mutter of the third bomb.

He had walked a mile or so when the moon rose into a clear sky, and soon he could distinguish the pale gleam of canal water off to the left. Then came a village, a place in which narrow sand-strewn alleys plunged darkly from the main road, lined with high, white-walled houses. Here Rule bought a bottle of violently coloured cordial water and half a scrawny fried chicken at a street stall illuminated by the harsh, thin light of a single acetylene flare.

Two miles beyond this place he noticed a small dot of red light motionless in the shimmer of moonlight.

It seemed to be off to the left of the road. He kept his eyes on it as he walked until, approaching closer, he could make out a splash of light around it, a circle of white-painted steel, and finally, the shape of a small covered truck. A red cross was painted on the side and a woman knelt near the off-side front wheel.

She looked up at the sound of his footsteps. He was shocked, so his heart thumped, when he first saw her face, which was strongly lighted by a portable trouble lamp clipped to the battery under the open bonnet. Large blue eyes, weary and despairing, looked up at him from a face marred by what seemed hundreds of small and large cuts and scratches. Some of this cross-hatching of injury still bled slightly, so her long fair hair was stained darkly at each brow.

"English?" he asked.

She shook her head.

"No. Australian. Can you help me, please?"

"You must get to a doctor as soon as possible and get those seen to."

"I am a doctor. My face isn't as bad as it looks—please don't be alarmed. Most of this is superficial, it won't kill me. But I've got people in there who're real problems."

She nodded towards the back of the ambulance, and went on:

"What can I do to get it up again? I must get them somewhere where they can be treated properly."

This meant nothing to him until she moved the trouble lamp so it lighted the front off-side of the vehicle, then he saw that the wheel and tyre were off, and that the whole weight of the truck rested on the brake-drum. Rule took the lamp and looked more closely. Near the cab door a sheetmetal jack was in position, but now flat on the ground, its spigot twisted around almost forty-five degrees. The ambulance had moved forward then, twisting the jack as the front axle fell.

"You should have used the handbrake," he said mildly. "Even if the engine'd been in gear this wouldn't have happened."

She nodded.

"I know. I'm a fool about things ·like that. It seemed such a crisis, having to stop and change the wheel. I panicked. Then, when it fell off the jack"—she stopped speaking abruptly, as though struck dumb. Looking at her more closely, he realised that she was in a state of shock, possibly quite severe.

He took her hand. It was shaking, and he tightened his grip until that stopped.

"I shouldn't worry. It seems to have toppled off fairly quietly, and on soft ground." He tried to make his voice calm and reassuring.

"You can fix it then. It's not damaged—not altogether?"

"We can see. First that jack must come out—then maybe it won't be too hard to straighten it."

He dropped the spare wheel in front of the axle and, using a balk of wood over it and under the chassis, levered the truck up so the brake-drum cleared the ground by three inches.

"Hold this down," he told her, "and I'll get the jack out. Good . . . The toolbox? Is there one?"

There was, and it included an engineer's hammer. Half a dozen blows of this straightened the mild steel jack enough to be serviceable.

"So far, fair enough," he said. "Now this time slip her into reverse gear and get that handbrake on good and hard."

Within five minutes the ambulance was back on its four wheels.

"Now you'll want to be on your way," he said briskly. "Good luck."

"And what about you? On a hiking tour, I suppose."

He grinned at this.

"In a way. My car went out of action some way back—and it was something not so easily fixed. I thought I'd do better on foot."

"Not any more. I might need you again."

He noticed with relief that now she spoke with more spirit. Her morale was restored to some extent.

"Well, I don't mind being commandeered," he replied lightly, smiled, and joined her in the ambulance cab. She set her teeth, let in the clutch with a bang and the truck leaped back into the traffic stream. Certainly a girl of character, he reflected. In spite of the squealing tyres and blaring horns behind, that was undoubtedly the only way of getting back on to the road.

"My name's Rule . . . Michael Rule," he said after a few minutes' silence.

"Jean Marsden," she responded abruptly. Her nerves were strung taut—nothing surprising about that. She said nothing for perhaps a minute, staring intently at the pool of light thrown ahead by the lamps, then spoke again:

"I was working in a hospital, you know, a small place in Cairo looking after poor people. It was mostly backed by the Society of Friends."

"You're a Quaker?"

"No, but I like all of them I've met. They're decent as individuals and also as a group, which is much rarer. They care about what happens to human beings—they don't like murder in the name of one-eyed ideologies and a lousy, make-believe sense of duty . . ." There was quiet venom in her slow, apparently dispassionate words.

"What happened there tonight?" she asked a few moments later. Now her voice was listless.

"Atom bombs."

"You're sure?"

"Quite certain. There's nothing else that could possibly give that kind of effect. It wasn't ordinary high explosive."

"That's horrible. Most people got to feeling it would never happen after all—I know I did. But it was a fools' paradise, wasn't it? If the thing is there, it only becomes a matter of time . . .

"Now I understand about our patients . . . those terrible burns! They were outside, you see, they must have been facing the explosion. We had all our women, twelve of them, out on the verandah ward. It was so warm this afternoon we'd rolled up the canvas blinds, so they must have been directly exposed to the blast."

"And you," he prompted, "you were at the hospital too?"

"No, I wasn't. I'd gone home for dinner to my flat—almost a mile from the hospital. It's at the back of the building, so I didn't see the flash, just a very bright, white reflected light. That was bad enough. I couldn't see anything for several minutes afterwards. Then I found the blood was dripping from my face. All the windowpanes had disappeared, and it must have been the tiny bits of flying glass that did this to my face. Then I got back into the ambulance—I'd been using it for transport over the mealtime—and drove back to the hospital."

"You went back?" he echoed.

"Why not? I hadn't the least idea what'd happened. I thought there might've been an Israeli air-raid, that I'd be needed urgently at the hospital. I don't mind saying I was scared. Then as I got closer I saw people wandering about in a dazed kind of way, some of them burned bright red and cut about. I stopped feeling afraid because I got so angry—just ordinary men and women, and children, injured like that . . .

"There wasn't much traffic about, and I got back to the hospital in a few minutes. It was right on the edge of the badly-damaged part of the city. There seemed to be fires burning everywhere, big fires, some of them, and when I looked out from the upper floor of the hospital the city . . . the houses . . . it was just like some kid's toy something monstrous had trodden on and kicked about.

"There was smoke everywhere and a weird kind of electric smell . . . you know, like you get around high-voltage switching stations, in the subway and places like that. It was very quiet most of the time, but in the distance you could hear flames crackling— and people crying out for help."

She stopped abruptly, and he waited silently for her to go on.

"The top verandah floor, where the men patients had been, had fallen in. I saw a couple of men, dead. The rest had just disappeared. There was nobody else about—I don't know what happened to the nurses and duty sister, and the children. Maybe they thought they had to get the children away first. So I got the women . . . all I could manage, all I could take . . . into the truck, and I came away."

"How many?"

"Six. The back of the truck has stretchers that slide in and out on rails. I could only bring the ones that could walk, and after I got them into the stretchers I gave them all heavy sedation. Later on, maybe in the morning, we'd better stop and I'll look at them again."

She shook her head, as though trying to banish some persistent and unpleasant mental picture.

"They're pretty bad, some of them," she went on. "It's not so much that they're severely cut. And there are no broken bones, nothing like that. But the burns . . . I've never seen anything like them before.

And even the women who seem to have just light injuries, they're dazed, they seem only half alive. I can't make it out . . . but what about you? You don't seem much hurt."

"One very small glass cut on the arm," Rule replied. "I was lucky. My flat's right on the outside of the city. I saw the flash indirectly, the way you did, there was a certain amount of broken glass, and that was it. The building was hardly damaged."

"What were you doing in Cairo?"

"I was at the British Embassy."

"You didn't stay to get in touch with the other people there."

"No." He paused for a moment. "I realised right from the start it was an atomic explosion, and that it'd be pretty well hopeless to try to get across the city. None of our people lived near me. If there are any still alive, there's nothing I can do to help them."

There was an awkward pause, then she asked:

"You're trying to get to Alex?"

"I suppose so. Anywhere I can get out of the country from. I want to find some hole in the corner—preferably useful—back in Britain—that's if it's still there, of course. There's no way of knowing what's happening elsewhere, is there? By the way, when we meet up with Egyptian officials, I'd as soon not have it known I'm a British diplomat."

"Then you'd better be something else—something definite."

"A tourist then. That makes for a background that gives plenty of scope for lying . . . Now, you look very tired. What about letting me drive for a while?"

"Not yet. If we stopped it mightn't be easy to get back into the traffic. Besides, it gives me something to think about. I need that."

He noticed the shake in her voice, and lapsed into silence. The line of traffic moved on steadily until the first haze of daylight showed up. As always during a long night drive Rule's ears and imagination played tricks, in which strange sounds, even a kind of lulling music, seemed to grow out of the neutral purr of the engine and the whine of the transmission. Then, as the light broadened he thought he heard other sounds. A few minutes later they came again, louder this time, clearly audible above the mechanical noises, low moans, sobs, then sharp cries of pain. They came from the back of the truck. He glanced uneasily at Jean.

"We'll have to stop," she said abruptly. "The sedation's wearing off."

She pulled the truck off the road, had the door open and was out of the ambulance immediately it stopped moving. Rule followed and watched as she unzipped the rear tarpaulin. He stepped forward to help as she struggled to move one of the stretchers, which had twisted sideways and locked its rollers. With one person on each side they were at last able to dislodge it, roll it outwards, and swing down the adjustable steel legs.

The woman in the stretcher moved constantly, contracting and extending her body and limbs with a terrible restlessness, accompanied by an unrestrained and piteous weeping, just like that of a young baby. Rule's blood chilled as she turned a dreadful face towards his, so badly burned, a dark livid red, that he was almost overcome by his nausea. The eyebrows and hair had been scorched off and loose skin was hanging from the brow.

Then the woman began to mutter, incomprehensibly to Rule, but Jean listened attentively, then took a small thermos flask of water and carefully poured it, a few drops at a time, between the woman's disfigured lips, through which her teeth shone, large and white.

"She used to be pretty. She was always laughing," Jean said in a voice she struggled to keep low and controlled. "Her name is Yasmin—"

. . . but by thy bed I kneel to pray, O Yasmin . . . Rule recollected, and shuddered . . .

"—she's eighteen. She'd only been in hospital a few days, after her third child was born. Now, I suppose the child's dead anyway. There's nothing I have I can treat this with . . . perhaps picric acid . . ." and she began to laugh, in a way that made Rule feel afraid. "Picric acid! As if—"

And then suddenly she seemed to take a grip on herself.

"All I can do is this."

And she took the hypodermic, gently pressed it into the woman's arm, and a few moments later, withdrew it. The pethedine took effect, and a semblance of peace returned to the ruined face.

"You've plenty of that, I hope," he said, his voice hoarse. "We'll need it, I think."

The horror grew as they withdrew the other stretchers, one at a time, and treated the remaining women. Two seemed to be only lightly injured, with no signs, on their hands and faces at least, of more than superficial burns. Yet even these, Rule noticed, seemed to have an insatiable thirst. He thought he knew what this meant, but could not bring himself to say anything. In any case, what purpose could it serve?

The woman they treated last was in the worst state. She moved only slightly, although it seemed that pain was driving her to a maximum possible exertion, and uttered only a very faint, regular moan. When Jean turned back the sheet Rule could see that the blast of heat radiation had ravaged her whole body. Her nipples had melted into blunt, charred cones. Blackened fragments of clothing stuck to her flesh, and, due to the quality of white objects repelling some of the heat from the bomb, a pattern from her underclothing had been printed on to the skin.

Rule shook his head to and fro, at first unable to speak.

"Bastards. Bastards. Bastards," at last he murmured over and over. Jean's eyes had filled with tears.

"That's what it does to people," she said quietly. "There were worse cases in the hospital—"

Suddenly her control vanished and she took his hands with an intense grip, staring at him, her eyes wide open, and glazed with blind panic.

"Much worse . . ." she went on, her voice rising. "Their whole faces had melted away . . . eyes, noses had gone and they could only just mumble. They complained they couldn't see . . ." Her voice was on the edge of hysteria, and he gripped her hands more tightly. "I looked at them . . . those empty eye-sockets . . . Then there was another one. She was lying back in the bed, quite peacefully. She tried to smile at me . . . then I took her hands . . . tried to lift her up in the bed, and do you know what happened . . . all her skin came away . . . like gloves! Like gloves, can you imagine that?" And she burst into hysterical laughter.

He shook her hard, then pulled her close to him. He could feel her body quiver and contort. Then came another torrent of weeping.

That's best . . . that's best . . . he thought silently, and waited. Slowly her emotion subsided. She drew away from him, almost as if affronted, and went to sit down on a low railing at the bridge approach, apathetically watching the passing traffic. Rule busied himself for the time being with necessary checks on the car battery, the oil, and the cooling water. Then he went back to her.

"Feeling better?"

"A little."

He groped in his mind for words to say.

"Of course you could never forget that. Nobody could. But it's happened, and it's in the past now. You've got to come to terms with it. Thank God you're alive yourself."

"I suppose so." Her voice was listless, and he doubted whether she had really heard him. He did his best to voice an anger and impatience he was far from feeling.

"Anyway, you've a job to do. Forget what happened in Cairo and have some thought for these women. You have a responsibility to them. You've got to keep them alive."

"Yes," she replied quietly, turning her mind to this line of thought. "What you say is true. If only we can keep them going ... not long now, until we reach Alex, is it?"

"And there'll be proper hospitals, proper treatment for them there," he said briskly, wondering if this would really be so.

She got up.

"Come on then. We'll have to hurry. But we'd better stop every two hours. I'll give them more water, more sedatives if necessary. I don't want them to feel any pain."

But when they stopped two hours later, just past the Nile crossing at Kafr el Zaiyat, two of the women were dead. One was the woman with very severe body burns, but the other had seemed to have only superficial injuries and Jean had been more confident of saving her than any of the rest.

"Why?" he asked, turning to her.

She shook her head.

"I think I know. It must be the radiation—not heat, but neutrons and gamma rays. They go deep, and damage internal cells without anything showing."

The nature of the external injuries on the four surviving patients was also changing ominously. The skin was sloughing off the burns, which were beginning to suppurate. Rule swung the ambulance back on to the road with a vicious jab at the accelerator. The traffic was thinner now and he took the risk, from time to time, of sounding the horn and overtaking slower vehicles ahead, for some traffic, mostly military, was now travelling in the opposite direction.

The Red Cross markings helped them when, at last, early in the afternoon, they crossed Maryut Lake and ran into the outskirts of Alexandria. Some sort of relief organisation was in existence here, for soldiers standing at crossroads directed them through the streets until they reached a broad, dusty compound on which perhaps a hundred tents had been pitched. They drove through the gate and stopped at a guardpost just inside, at which a tall, greying man with an air of authority approached them.

"English, English, are you?" he said. "Very well. This is the reception area. I am the doctor in charge here. How many patients?"

"Four still living," Rule answered, "but they're very sick. They need urgent attention."

The doctor nodded curtly.

"We'll do what is possible for them."

Rule went with him to the back of the truck, where the doctor inspected the motionless forms one by one. Then he shook his head.

"These women are all dead."

"That can't be!" Jean cried out, running forward.

"Dead. Yes, all dead," the Egyptian doctor responded heavily. "Don't blame yourself, young miss. So far we've had two thousand people admitted to this emergency hospital alone, and it's only one of twenty, maybe more, in the city." His voice rose. "Do you know how many of those two thousand have died already? Nearly thirteen hundred! It's the radiation, there's nothing we can do.

71

"Later, many of those now seeming healthy will also go down with radiation sickness. It will be a less severe form, but bad enough. A few of these we shall save, but these terrible burned ones . . ." He shook his head.

Another vehicle pulled in behind them. Its horn sounded urgently and the doctor moved towards it. He had already forgotten them.

Six

Ten minutes later Rule stopped the ambulance outside the quiet suburban bungalow that housed the British Consulate. To his surprise the white-painted pole on the front lawn carried no flag, and there was no answer to his repeated knocking on the closed door. He tried the handle. The door was locked.

Finally a key clicked and an elderly man, perhaps a gardener or caretaker, opened the door and looked out at them. He did not trouble to conceal his hostility.

"I'd like to see Mr. Edwards, please," Rule said.

The man spat on the ground at his feet.

"Not here," he said in heavily-accented English. "Not come back. Has gone. This morning."

With these few phrases Rule had to be content, for the man turned his back, went inside and slammed the door. They returned to the ambulance. A small sedan was parked behind it that had not been there when they came in. A fair, stout man at its wheel glanced nervously up and down the street, then beckoned to them.

"You're English?" he asked abruptly. "Of course. Well, get in, will you, so we can go."

"Is there really such a hurry?" Rule asked mildly. "Besides, we do have our own transport."

The man in the car shook his head impatiently.

"And very conspicuous it is, too. All our diplomatic people were flown out this morning. Now they're watching the consulate, with the idea of picking up any British nationals who go there. I was amazed they didn't get you just now—the gendarmes must be away for their cup of coffee or whatever. But somebody would tell them about your white ambulance with its red crosses and you wouldn't get far."

He peered at Jean and then changed his tone.

"Sorry. My name's Rendrick, by the way, Matthew Rendrick. I'm the B.O.A.C. rep. here."

"That's fine. I'm Michael Rule. This is Dr. Jean Marsden. From Cairo. You're just the man we want. If it can be fixed, we'll take the next plane out."

Rendrick laughed explosively.

"The next plane out goes straight to Moscow—and the next, and the rest after that. The Russians have taken over here, and very methodical they are, too. There's no obvious way in or out for any British or American nationals. Now will you come, before we're all behind bars?"

Rule blinked, then opened the back door for Jean without another word. Rendrick barely waited for the door to close before he backed the car away from the ambulance and pulled out into the street.

"One small point—why are you still here?" Rule asked.

"I wish I weren't, but it's a good question. The fact is I was off on a trip down the coast birdwatching, and I came back a few hours too late. Don't grin. I'm a spare-time ornithologist and marsh birds are my specialty.

"So far as I can gather they gave European and American nationals just three hours to get out. The last aircraft was at noon. I found this out at my office. When I got there at two, it was on the point of closing down, with the last of my local staff going home. Now I'm on my way home, but when I saw you two at the consulate it occurred to me you might not know the score. So I stuck my beak in."

"Thanks for that. You might also tell us what's happening generally. Is there a world war? What in the devil happened in Cairo?"

"No war yet—that's according to the B.B.C. I heard a broadcast on the office radio just before I left. As for Cairo, the story being given out is that a secret society of Israeli army officers got hold of some atomic field weapons—small things—smuggled them into the city and set the fuses, or whatever it is for nuclear weapons."

"Small, you said?" Jean asked, and there was something in her voice that made him glance quickly around at her.

"You were in Cairo when this happened? That would be bloody, to put it mildly."

Jean did not reply, and Rule said quickly: "It was all of that and more for her. We'll tell you later—it's a long nasty story. The real point just now is what do we do next?—sit about and wait for the Russians to pick us up?"

"Or the Gippos to tear us to bits, more like," Rendrick said grimly. "There isn't much love here for the Western world, believe me. Things were bad enough before, but now . . . No, we have to get out of the country somehow. I reckon it'll be safe enough for us all to stay at my house tonight—it's a quiet, out-of-the-way place, the neighbours aren't close and I think I can trust my servants for a while. As soon as possible we'll see what's what. The best way could be to buy a small native boat, a fishing craft or a *felucca*, and quietly disappear out to sea in that."

"Provided we knew where we were going," Rule said.

"I can take care of that. I've sailed a lot in small craft in these waters, and I think I have the right contacts to get a boat from someone who'd keep his mouth shut. It's a long way to any safer place, of course, it's not a trip I'd suggest if I could think of any other way out. Movement overland is obviously quite out of the question."

Rendrick had been patiently threading his way through denser traffic as they negotiated the business centre of the city. There was a break in the row of buildings, and the blue waters of the Mediterranean, startling after the drab colours of the land, came into view.

"Sorry for all this toing and froing," Rendrick remarked. "I'm taking back streets where I can, and avoiding places where I know there'll be police on point duty."

However, they made better speed as the car turned east into the coast road, Rue al-Geish, and the city thinned out. The sea was in sight most of the time, and they passed a string of beach resorts on their left. Finally Rendrick turned off towards the sea, along a short, narrow lane. It ended at a gate in a seven foot high plastered wall, covered with vines, behind which palms waved gently in the cool northerly breeze, their leaves sharp and distinct against the clear blue sky. Rendrick drove inside, then closed and bolted the gates again. Rule looked about him curiously.

"A pleasant spot."

Rendrick nodded.

"I shall be sorry to leave it. I had myself well organised here, I feel—better than in a flat in the city."

The small, well-kept garden gave directly on to the sea, and the square flat-roofed cream stucco house, with a big pergola along its northern side, was set on the edge of a sandy beach. A Moth sailing skiff was drawn up on a small concrete yard, sheltered under a thatched roof, its long spruce mast sticking out from one end. The house might have had no neighbours—certainly no other building was visible from inside its garden walls.

The interior was cool and dark, and it was some minutes before Rule could take in his surroundings. They were those of a man with many interests, mostly intellectual and contemplative. There was a large stack of shelves carrying hundreds of books, an old Bechstein grand piano, a modern harpsichord, and a comprehensive record and tape playing system. Rather too many photographs and sketches of birds decorated the walls, and on a side-table was a stuffed ibis-like bird, coloured a modest blue-black and white, but remarkable for a halo of pink feathers over its head.

"Crowned crane," Rendrick said briefly, when he noticed Rule glance at it.

"You'll be leaving a lot behind here."

"No use crying over it. Dr. Marsden. That's the way to the bathroom. In the cabinet there ought to be some things that'll help you with those cuts on your face. There's a less palatial shower out here, Rule, but you'll manage. Join me out front when you're ready."

He spoke with the terse, almost cross manner of the kind-hearted man whom experience has taught not to show that quality too freely. Rule knew the type, and considered that this was someone they could depend on.

When he came back to the group of wicker chairs on the flagged terrace under the pergola, Jean Marsden had already joined Rendrick. Her face was certainly cleaner, and its injuries less startling.

"Feeling better?" he asked. "You look it. Not quite time yet, I'd say, to have your picture taken, but there's nothing that won't mend in a day or two."

"I'm dog-tired," she said with feeling. "I like this place. I think I'll stay a month or two."

Rendrick smiled indulgently.

"You might as well drink up," he said, indicating a

well-filled drink cabinet on wheels that he had rolled out onto the terrace. "We can't take it with us, and it'll help you to think about the bad news."

"Just general bad news, or something specific?" Rule asked.

"Specific. All my servants have gone."

"Too bad. Perhaps they've taken the day off, seeing you weren't here."

"Unfortunately not. There's always at least one of them about, regardless of days off. I've looked out in their quarters and there's no doubt about it, they've packed up and gone. Yesterday, or even this morning, I suppose."

"No notes or explanations?"

"Not a thing." He poured himself another drink. "I don't like it. They wouldn't all leave, just like that, without a good reason. This place is their home—some of them have been here longer than I have, and that's seven years. They went because someone told them to go—someone they didn't dare say no to."

"The police."

"I expect so. Deduction, we must make our move sooner than I'd thought. We aren't safe here for long. Obviously, the police went away when they found I wasn't here—but they'll be back."

"So they're better organised than you'd thought." Rendrick nodded.

"I keep forgetting it's Russians, and not Egyptians, who're organising things now. I suppose they kept a careful check on who left in the aircraft and who didn't, and they're methodically following up."

"What would happen if they did find us here?" Jean asked.

"That depends, doesn't it? If they didn't like the look of our faces, it'd be easy enough to charge us with spying. On that one people don't come to court quickly or get out of prison easily. So my advice to you, if it's needed, is that if the police do come back soon—now, for instance—be as pleasant and co-operative as possible. Gentle like the lamb. No injured feelings, no banging the table."

"Agreed," Rule said quietly. "And in fact there is someone out there now."

Unlike the other two, he was facing outward, towards the lawn and the sea.

Rendrick got up from his deep cane chair with surprising agility for one so short and rotund. Then, as he turned and saw the slight, dejected-looking figure standing near the boatshed, he relaxed.

"One of your people?" Rule asked.

"The one I'd hoped most of all to see. It'd be difficult to get hold of a suitable boat without him, but probably it'll be easy if he and his family'll help. Fuad's the son of one of the fishermen who moor in the east harbour. He's been coming here two or three days a week for years, working in the garden, giving the Moth a coat of paint, odd jobs like that. Two or three years ago his family were in a touchy financial position and I was able to help them. They'll help me now . . . Get yourselves another drink, will you, while I talk to him."

The conversation took some time, and it was plain even out of earshot that Fuad was uneasy, even afraid. Rule and Jean watched—Rendrick was waving his arms to emphasise some argument, while Fuad nodded solemnly. The contrast between them, as they stood together on the lawn, was almost ludicrous. Apart from the fact that they were of about the same height, two human beings could scarcely have differed more.

"Your opinion of Rendrick?" Rule asked Jean abruptly.

She nodded, a quick, intelligent movement.

"I like him. He's genuine, and he'll stick by us, I'm sure, while we need him. Also, it's to his advantage. There's safety in numbers. And nobody can sail a boat far, can they, by themselves—not unless it's a rather special boat?"

"I hadn't thought that far ahead," Rule said slowly. "But you're right, of course."

"What worries me," she persisted, "is whether his ideas are reasonable. I'm right out of my element with this talk of small boats. I can't even swim."

Rule pursed his lips.

"It's not the best time of year. The north winds can cut up rather badly. One tends to think of the Med as a sort of pond, a place where it's always calm and balmy, but that's far from true in winter. The point is, is there anything else we could do, anywhere else we could go? You might volunteer to work in a hospital, I suppose, and that could get you by. On the other hand, even taking an optimistic view of the future, I think we'd be much better clean out of the country."

A spasm of pain crossed her face.

"Perhaps I'm a coward," she said. "Probably I'm letting down people who need help badly, but I couldn't face any more of that—watching people die like those women did. Am I a coward? Should I go back and work in one of those hospitals?"

"I think you'd be mad to do it, but the real decision has to rest with you. Would you feel badly about things, about yourself, in future, if you didn't?"

"You have an unusual approach to people," she said slowly. "No, I don't believe it would matter to me now. Perhaps I have what's supposed to be a female vice, I'm too subjective. Now my own patients have died, I don't care much about the rest. They've got their own doctors, and the Russians, to look after them. I've always tried to be honest with myself, and that's how I feel. I'll come with you, if you'll have me."

"Of course I'll have you," he said, with a shade

more emphasis than his voice usually carried. She glanced across to him curiously, then looked away as he met her eyes. Rendrick came back then, and sat down again.

"Pretty much as I'd expected," he explained. "The police were here late this morning. If I'd been a few hours earlier I'd have been in the bag. They harangued the servants, told them I was now an enemy of the people, subject to arrest if I came back. On no account were they to go on working for me. They could apply for new jobs at the labour exchange.

"But there are one or two bright patches in the situation, all the same. My old cook-lady, bless her—she can't cook—used her presence of mind and let the police worm the information out of her that I'd be back here about noon on Tuesday. Fuad says he's sure the police believed this. That gives us almost two days, provided the house isn't being watched, and I don't think it is. Nor does Fuad. He knows the lie of the land pretty well around here, and he had a good look about before he came—for his own sake.

"The other important thing is that Fuad already has a boat available—she belongs to his family—that they'd be willing to let us have. I can buy her outright with local money in cash I'm holding here. It's useless to me now in any case. She's a native craft, which is best for us. If we're going to make a cruise that's in effect an illegal exit from the country, the less conspicuous we are the better."

Rule nodded.

"When can we have the boat?"

"I've told Fuad it has to be as soon as possible— some time tomorrow. At the moment it's unlikely the police will be back before Tuesday, but I'm sure they can be expected then. If they find the place empty they'll probably just assume I never came back. On that basis it doesn't seem to matter how late we leave."

"Provided it's before Tuesday."

"Of course. But on the other hand it would be impossible to keep our going a complete secret. Fuad and his family won't talk, but there's every chance of other fishermen seeing us when we put to sea unless we actually leave at night, and I regard that as too dangerous. We'll need the best possible conditions until we settle down to sailing the boat. That won't be easy. One of the things that's worrying me is how well we'll be able to handle the sort of craft I'm expecting. Most of them are operated on the basis of having any amount of crew scrambling about. The gear is primitive—no winches, double blocks, and labour-saving gadgets like that."

"Can't we use a crew?"

Rendrick shook his head.

"I asked Fuad about that. He didn't even like discussing it, and in the end he made it plain nobody would take the risk. It'd amount to helping us escape, and if they were caught they could get into bad trouble over that. Fuad's family are sticking out their necks quite far enough just by letting us have the boat. By the way, if we're caught, the story must be that we stole her, so they won't be implicated. Even granted all that, it's important for us to keep their goodwill, and I didn't like to press the crew issue too hard. Do either of you sail?"

Both Jean and Rule shook their heads, and Rendrick sighed.

"I'll just have to see you learn quickly. Well, what about it? Do we take the boat and have a try?"

"We get the boat," Rule said without hesitation.

"Dr. Marsden?"

"Jean, please. Yes, we get the boat."

Seven

Dawn next day was fine, with a light, chilly breeze. The *felucça* was already lying to her anchor off the beach, nodding and dipping on the wavelets that broke with small, hollow roars on the sand.

"Fuad towed her along last night," Rendrick said. "And I've paid him. Thus far, fair enough, and it's on the credit side, too, that she's just like thousands of other small craft in the delta. On the other hand, she's a Nile river boat, not really built for the open water, rather old, too, although she seems sound enough by local standards. She's beamy, very bluff, plenty of freeboard up front but practically nothing elsewhere. I don't fancy her for heavy weather, but she should manage even that carefully handled."

The white-painted hull was broad, some eight feet in the beam and perhaps twenty-eight feet long, with a sheerline rising sharply to a curved, well-shaped bow. The short, heavy mast was stepped, and stayed with heavy, rusting ploughsteel wire rope crudely secured with U bolt connectors. The much longer boom of her lateen rig, the sail already laced to it, was lying lengthwise in the hull. The *felucca* was open, except for six feet or so of deck forward, with broad thwarts in the stern and amidships, scarred with hundreds of cuts from fishing knives.

"She'll get us there," Rendrick concluded, after looking her over for a few minutes.

"And where is 'there'?"

"That depends on the wind. I had toyed with the idea of standing pretty much to the north and crossing open sea to the south coast of Cyprus—say Limassol, but that's a good two hundred and fifty miles, and the way the wind's held lately, we'd have to beat into it every inch of the way. No trouble to a modern racing yacht, but these native craft are much happier off the wind, especially with the kind of crew we amount to. Closehauled I doubt we'd average better than three and a half knots—we'd be at sea for three days, maybe more."

"And the alternatives?"

"There aren't many. It pretty much chooses itself, don't you agree? Greece, Sicily, anywhere up that way, would take us a week or more, if we ever made it. There's only desert westward. It has to be Israel, one of the fishing villages over the other side of the canal. Somewhere around El Arish—and we'll just have to hope nobody's persuaded the Israelis to pull out of Sinai yet. That'd be about two hundred miles, but if the wind stays the way it's been the last few days, it should be feasible. These *feluccas* make a reasonable speed reaching, and if we got away as soon as possible we'd be well on our way before I was missed. As to that, there's a better than fifty-fifty chance they'll never know how I got away, and care even less. I'm not that important a Briton after all—just a humble booking-clerk type."

He grinned engagingly and added without emphasis: "How about you two? Nobody's going to be breathing down your necks?"

"I can't absolutely guarantee it," Rule said. "On the other hand there's only the smallest possible chance that any officials who'd be interested even know I'm here, or who I am."

"Something I also do not want to know," Rendrick broke in quickly.

"There's no mystery, I'm not on any special

mission. It's just that under some circumstances I could be a useful prisoner to them and a bloody nuisance to our own government."

Rendrick nodded.

"We oughtn't to waste time then. We'll have to beat northward fairly much so we can give the lee shore and the Damietta Banks a healthy offing. We could be intercepted off Port Said if they were wise to us and felt they wanted any of us badly enough. The boat's stocked with food and water, and she's as ready as possible in other respects. We haven't time to give her a major refit, and there's little point in anything that stops short of that.

"The earlier we get away the fewer curious folk'll be watching. That's why I dragged you from your beds so early. I'll take the dinghy out now and get the sail on her. You be ready in half an hour."

However, he was back looking for them in less than fifteen minutes.

"Sorry, it takes two men to get that thumping great spar up. You'd better come along now."

Even with two it was difficult. The halyard was rove through a single block that had rusted solid in its housing at the masthead. It took their combined efforts to raise the thirty-foot boom with its burden of heavy, greying canvas. Halfway up the mast it began to swing and thrash about alarmingly in the freshening breeze. The *felucca* shuddered and the mast shrouds twanged with the strain.

"Hold it there," Rendrick shouted, and dived for the tackrope of the sail, securing it to a heavy iron ringbolt on the stemhead. The foot of the sail thus secured, it was more docile, and five minutes more saw the boom in place across the top of the mast.

"Cast off the dinghy," Rendrick told Rule.

"Don't we take it? It could come in handy."

Rendrick hesitated for a moment, then shook his head.

"We're better off without it. It's too big to get inboard and towing it would slow us down too much. No, get rid of it. Next thing, there's some kind of anchor down below. Take in the slack, and haul up when I tell you."

However the *felucca* over-ran the mooring and the sail was taken aback as Rule struggled without effect to break the anchor free of the bottom.

"It's only sand down there. What the hell?" Rendrick said peevishly. "You'd better lend a hand, Jean. And hurry it up. If we put on a comedy turn here every fisherman down the beach'll remember us when the police start asking questions."

Rule accepted this in silence, but grunted when finally they had a rusty, dripping mass of ancient gear wheels, water pipe, and fencing wire hove up short under the gunwale.

"They don't go in for refinements here," Rendrick commented. "If it works and it's cheap—preferably costs nothing at all—it'll do."

The *felucca* was already making good progress, the sail setting and drawing well in spite of its patches, darns, and mildew stains.

"You can take her," Rendrick told Rule when they were half a mile off the beach.

"The only boat I've ever handled was a dinghy with an outboard motor."

"Then now's the time to learn. I can't sit here day and night. This rope—the mainsheet—is the only one you need worry about, and the tiller. Remember, whatever way you move the tiller, the boat turns in the opposite direction. Keep the mainsheet with a bit of slack, so the foot of the sail's just above the gunwale.

"You'll find that left to herself she'll round up into the wind and stop. All good boats do that. You have to adjust the rudder so she can't round up, but at the same time keep her as close into the wind as possible.

If the sail starts to flap turn a little downwind. If in doubt, or a sudden squall comes up, just let both tiller and mainsheet go. The boat'll look after herself then."

Rule found that in this moderate, steady breeze handling the *felucca* wasn't too difficult. With her long shallow keel she responded placidly to inexpert rudder movements. They made good progress, so that when the sun rose into a cloudless sky the point of Abu Qîr was close by to starboard and the sea already taking on a deeper brown from the Nile waters emerging at the Rosetta Mouth. The low coastline almost faded from sight as they crossed the wide bay outside Buheirat el Idku, becoming clear and distinct again at the mouth of the big river. This passed, Rendrick took the tiller again, eased the mainsheet a foot, and brought the *felucca* around until the wind was almost abeam. As the morning wore on they met a score of other small craft, but the occupants of these seemed taken up with their own affairs, seldom sparing the *felucca* so much as a glance as they passed.

Along the monotonous sandy ribbon of coast that divides the big lake of Buheirat el Burullus from the sea this traffic thinned, until they were completely alone. The coast, still in sight, was only a low line of sandhills, unrelieved by any signs of life. With afternoon the wind rose slightly and a distinct chop cut up on the shallow water, through which the *felucca* pushed her bluff bows in a mist of spray. Towards sunset Rendrick closehauled her again to get a better offing before nightfall. Long before darkness closed in, the land had dropped below the horizon.

"There'll be a moon in an hour or two, and more light to steer by. You can take over the tiller then, while I sleep. Until then, why don't you join her?" He nodded towards Jean, who was already asleep on a pile of old canvas under the forward deck. She did not stir as Rule lay down near her. For a while he quietly watched her face, which looked older and vulnerable in repose.

To his surprise a strong sense of concern for her touched him—a feeling he had never had for another human being, certainly not in such a personally involved way. Concern for others, compassion, even pity, had always been for him an intellectual response, based on reason, detached from himself, and, he had to admit, with more than a hint of a sense of his own superiority. The sudden wave of feeling for Jean was naked emotion, primitive, strong, and in a way, hurtful, yet the sexual curiosity that had stimulated his interest in particular women in the past was not yet evident. His need for her at once became evident as a total one, unable to be placed neatly in one compartment or another.

These feelings were not uniformly pleasant, including the overtones of annoyance, even mild alarm, that he usually experienced at the prospect of any involvement with another person. His mother had always seemed to him a cool, detached person, who had kept life at arm's length, and he had admired her very much. Just before he dropped into sleep a memory he had forgotten, and an echo of pain, returned to him.

He had been very young—was he yet at school? His mother had been away for the day and he had been left in the care of a servant, with no other child to play with. Time had seemed to stand eerily still. For a long time it had rained and he had waited, his nose pressed against the window, looking out through the streams of water pouring down the glass for his mother's return. When I've counted to ten, she'll come. No. All right, then I'll count again, this time up to eight . . .

Towards evening, she came. He ran to her at once, gripping her tightly around the legs, burying his face in her clothing. She seemed startled, gave a nervous little laugh, and pushed him away with a gesture of impatience.

"Silly," she said. "You'll crush my dress . . . but see here, I've brought you something."

It was a beautiful little model of a boat, but it was made entirely from china. All the tiny sails and spars were stiff and rigid. Nothing moved, so the boat was not interesting. It would be too heavy to float. For a while he looked at it, tinkering, while his mother went upstairs; then one of the fragile mizzen sails broke. He put the little model carefully on the mantelshelf and went outside. In the garden he drove some pigeons out of a tree. Satisfied, he watched them fly off, squawking in alarm. The dress then, was more important than he was. And the boat was no good. It wouldn't do anything, just break easily.

From then on he had approached his mother more formally. Most childhoods probably held a similar experience, teaching the lesson that too open, too unreserved an affection, might result in rebuff and hurt. He dropped into sleep.

It seemed only minutes before Rule felt a hand on his arm, and Rendrick's voice, at first a far-off echo, shouldered its way into his consciousness. He opened his eyes, got up, and looked around. A gibbous moon sat above the horizon, linked to the *felucca* by a broad track of light that shimmered and sparkled on the waves. The stars were pale against a blue satin sky. The wind had dropped considerably, and the *felucca* plashed her way eastward with a steady easy motion.

Rendrick yawned.

"Just keep her heading a little left of the moon. Wake me if you see anything, or the weather gets bad."

Rule glanced up at the dimly illuminated mass of the sail, which was filling well. The end of the boom described slow circles against the pattern of stars, the sound of the waves against the hull was peaceful and hypnotic. Beyond the low, broad, stern transom the wake boiled away in a pale stream, lit up from time to time by the cold fire of phosphorescence. From various parts of the boat her ancient hemp cordage creaked and muttered as it worked against the wooden spars.

He looked up at a slight sound. Jean was coming aft. She sat down on the stern thwart beside him.

"Can't you sleep?" he asked.

She shook her head.

"I've had enough. What's the time?"

He glanced at his watch.

"Just after twelve. "

"It's still early."

"Yes, but we're making good time. Another two days and a night like this, and we ought to be close to the Israeli coast. The day after that we should be in Tel Aviv."

"I expect so," she said flatly.

"You don't sound very happy about it."

"Don't I? I should be, I suppose. I had something to do before, and my whole life was fitted around just going on doing it. Now I don't like the idea of having to take the next step, of having to settle what it's going to be."

"Perhaps other things'll decide it for you."

"I hope so. That's cowardly though, isn't it? People always ought to know where they're going."

"Let it take its own time. There's plenty of room for good doctors, especially people like you who're prepared to help in out-of-the-way places."

"Maybe," she answered listlessly. "But I might go back home for a while if I can. I have some money banked in England. I should go and see my mother. She's not in the best of health."

"Where's home? Sydney?"

"It is Sydney really—a place called Parramatta, just west of Sydney city. Actually it's all just part of the one built-up area, there's no open country in between."

"Brothers and sisters?"

"One elder sister. She's married—lives in a country town called Bathurst. It's nice, much better than Sydney. Sydney's too big, it's strangling in its own smog and rubbish and everyone's trying to bring up kids in blocks of apartments with no gardens or anywhere to play. So they watch the telly from when they get home from school till when they go to bed and everyone's wondering why they grow up withdrawn, and don't say much.

"And I had a brother, three years younger than me. He was killed in Vietnam."

She shivered, and said: "It's getting colder."

"It always does after midnight, in the open air."

"You've spent a lot of nights in the open air?"

"A good many."

She shifted closer to him. He moved his free arm to put it around her, then hesitated as she seemed to flinch slightly.

"Put your arm there if you want," she then said quietly.

"Do you want?"

"I suppose I do."

She felt small and warm under his shoulder. He could feel her light, relaxed breathing and said nothing for a few minutes.

"It's horrible when someone you love dies," she said abruptly. "Of course, everyone knows that, but they don't really feel it till it happens to them. Rob—that's my brother—and I were very close. My sister's quite a lot older.

"He *shouldn't* have been killed—there again, everyone knows it's all hideous, stupid waste, young men getting killed like that, but we all go on doing it.

What are we trying to prove? I think it's just like those people who used to sacrifice their children by throwing them inside the god with a blazing fire inside. Somehow it made them feel better to do it."

"Baal," Rule said under his breath.

"Was that the one? Rob was a national serviceman, you know, that's the polite Australian term for a conscript. Like all the others he was called up when he was twenty and he hadn't been over there a month when he was killed with two others. More than half the Australians that were sent to Vietnam were conscripts—after the government found they couldn't get people to volunteer for love or money.

"One of Rob's mates who came back told me he loathed what they were forced to do to the village people. He said the Communists in Phuoc Tuy Province, that's where the Australians were—used to dig up the minefields our people laid. Then they'd use our own weapons back against the Australians. Quite a few of our boys got killed that way. It was all lousy and unfair. He told me our boys tried to do what they could to help the local people—building dams and schools and things like that—but it was no good. He said that when he passed a bunch of South Vietnamese village children, after a while he didn't like to turn round, because he'd be sure to find them spitting at him. Who the hell did the politicians think they were, sending our boys to put up with that sort of thing?

"Mind you, a lot of ordinary people felt we ought to keep in with the Americans, too. They felt the United States had saved our bacon during the Japanese war, and if there was trouble in future they'd be able to help us again. So we ought to help them in Vietnam."

"It's a point of view," Rule said.

"I suppose so. Our family thought that way until Rob got killed. Not that he, or we, ever really believed he would die. It always has to be someone else, not you. Of course it was a bore, getting the marble—less pay than his normal job, and that sort of thing."

"Marble?"

"Of course, you wouldn't know. We run all sorts of things, like hospitals, on the proceeds of lotteries. They even paid for the Sydney Opera House that way. All the clubs in New South Wales are financed mostly from people playing the poker machines—you'd call them fruit machines. So why not Vietnam?

"All the names of the nineteen-year-olds went into a great ballot. They drew it with marbles, just like the lottery. If the marble with your birthday came up, you were in the army for two years, with a fair chance of being sent to Vietnam. A lot of people were against it, of course—not just ratbags and Communists, but decent people who sometimes tried to think for themselves. They didn't like the ballot system, they didn't like the idea of conscripting young men in peacetime, they didn't like them being killed in Vietnam, and they didn't like the way so much world opinion turned against Australia.

"It was a fact that once you got under their skins most people were ashamed of the war, but not so many had the guts to say so. Australians don't like to be thought different from anyone else. Before they say anything they look over their shoulders to see who's listening."

"They're not alone in that," Rule said. "But I'm a bit surprised. We've always thought of Australians as healthy individualists. Great sportsmen, drink a lot of beer—characters, you know, and proud of it."

She laughed.

"And the rest! You might just have a point, though, about the beer. My people were pretty typical, an average couple. My father was a storeman in a big factory, he'd worked there for about fifteen years and they were paying off the house in Parramatta over twenty-five years. I did well at school and I think they regarded that as a bit queer. I got scholarships for higher secondary school, then university. My parents helped me, they were proud of me, but at the same time they were uneasy. Having a daughter training to be a doctor didn't go with that neighbourhood.

"Then when Rob got killed things went to bits in a hurry. My father died three months later, with heart trouble, they said. It was that all right. It was just too much for me. I got to hate everything, the government, the people around me, everyone going about their silly business as if nothing had happened.

"So I joined up with the Moratorium people—mostly students and trade unionists agitating against the war. I believed they were right. I still do for that matter. Towards the end of the war things got pretty bad. One procession I went in on May Day met up with a bad lot of police. Most of the police are OK, but everyone knows the worst are as bad as the crooks.

"That day we were picketing the United States Consulate—just standing about not doing much and thinking we were the wave of the future, when some of the police went for us with truncheons and pistol butts—our police carry guns. There wasn't any reason to break up that demo.—it was just like scores of others that hadn't been interfered with—but you could see they liked doing it. They were only cops and we were university students, a privileged class, I suppose they thought. Some of them had taken off the badges with their numbers on so they couldn't be identified afterwards. Then they laid into us—girls, too. And of course anyone who fought back or tried to resist was arrested for obstructing them."

"I didn't know things got as bitter as that in Australia."

"Well, one doesn't hear much about that kind of

thing, does one, unless it's on a very big scale. Even then, most people don't come in contact with it. I used to talk about the Nazis to German families, who'd migrated to Australia, and they all said they'd never actually seen anyone being beaten up or known anyone arrested by the Gestapo. And, of course—we found this out in Australia during the Vietnam war—people don't *want* to know. They'd rather not be aware of unpleasant things, even if they directly concerned them, things they should have been prepared to consider before they voted. And they get angry with people who try to remind them. It isn't right, is it?"

He shook his head.

"Most people think they've got enough personal problems of their own. It takes a lot to get them stirred up enough to do anything outside their own lives. Have you read any of Toynbee's books? The historian?"

"I've heard of him, but when you're doing medicine you don't have much time for reading anything else."

"He made a point that really amounts to saying it's the burnt child that dreads the fire. Nations that tend to be belligerent are often the ones that haven't recently known the effects of war on their own soil. In the ones that've been fought over in living memory people know about war—they're more careful. You need to be hurt to learn."

She looked up doubtfully.

"Maybe that had something to do with it. But most Australians are pretty good people, you know. They aren't vicious or power-mad, they're mostly law-abiding, they wouldn't see a cat hurt unnecessarily, and they always have their hands in their pockets for some good cause or another. No, I'm sure it's just that they don't want to know. They'd rather hide their heads in the sand. 'If I can't see it, it isn't there,' could be the national motto. That and 'don't rock the boat.' "

He laughed.

"And you're a born boat-rocker."

"D'you think so? A stirrer, they'd call it at home. Maybe I am. Anyway, I got sick of it all, and when I graduated I looked about straight away for anything that'd get me out of Australia. I found out about the Quakers and their hospital in Cairo, and that's how I got there . . .

"So that's all about me. I've been talking a lot about myself—it's your fault for listening. Most people don't. You get the feeling they're only half-hearing you, and waiting for you to stop talking so they can start. You're not like that, are you? I'd noticed that when you say something, it's for a reason. You aren't a small-talk man."

"Do you find that dull?"

"No, restful. What about me? You'll think I talk too much, not like an English girl. She'd be more withdrawn and reticent."

"You're a long way behind the times. English girls aren't like that any more. Most of them are mighty direct—too direct. It tends to make a man wary, being crowded."

"You're not married then?"

"Not even spoken for. As the years drift past one vaguely thinks it's the right thing to do, to get married. I've been close to it once or twice, but I didn't feel strongly enough about any of the girls when it came to the point. In the end I'd suddenly think . . . 'hell, this is you, Michael Rule, drifting towards the double bed.' "

She laughed.

"Like drifting on the rocks. Poor Michael! But you're right, of course. I wouldn't marry for the sake of it, only if I knew I just had to have him, that I couldn't do without him, not any way!"

"You've never felt that way about anyone? I'm surprised. You're an attractive girl."

"Do you think so? You haven't seen me at my best," she said soberly. "I reckon I look better at the moment when the light's rather poor. No, I never felt happy with the young men I knew. They were selfish—bed first, then questions and getting to know one another afterwards was their way, if they could get it. I found it off-putting. Female emotions aren't as"—she searched for the word—"as compartmentalised as that. Not mine, anyway. Maybe a man wants sex more than anything else from a woman, but it doesn't operate the other way, except perhaps for nymphomaniacs and people like that, and I reckon there aren't many of them. A man needs to understand that what a woman really wants is to be understood, to be looked after by someone who fundamentally seems to know what everything's about. Up to a point women trade sex for love."

"And you didn't find anyone understanding among the young radicals you got about with?"

"They were more selfish than any of the others when it came to the point. And they certainly didn't know what things were about. I suppose they were too young . . . You're from a very different background from me, aren't you?" she added suddenly.

"I suppose I am. D'you think that's important?"

"It probably is," she said thoughtfully, looking up at him gravely, "but it isn't everything."

"Sometimes—how do you do it?—you look about ten."

He tightened his grip on her.

"Do you usually cuddle and kiss ten-year-olds?" she said tartly.

"How did you know I wanted to kiss you?"

"Never mind. But don't, not just now."

"Why not?"

"Say . . . 'pretty please, with sugar on it'."

"Like hell!"

"I haven't made up my mind about you yet."

He started to laugh.

"And you don't know me," she insisted.

"What don't I know?"

"Lots of things. For instance, I have a bad temper, also I hate to admit I'm ever wrong. It's just the moonlight that makes you want to kiss me."

"Of course," he replied drily, "and propinquity. It's in all the books."

Eight

Jean was asleep again, still sitting beside him, when the wind veered and suddenly blew harder. The sail thrashed noisily as the *felucca* rounded up and lost way.

"What's up?"

Rendrick was awake. He looked briefly at the situation and grabbed the tiller. The *felucca*, in irons, was already making sternway, the sail flapping madly. Rendrick reversed the tiller and she slowly came back on to the wind and surged ahead, heeling until the water splashed over the lee gunwale. Rendrick looked back at the wake glimmering in the moonlight and eased the sheet a few inches.

"This'll help us on our way," he said. "But it's enough of a good thing. I hope it doesn't get any fresher."

But it did. The squall ushered in a strong gale, which shifted treacherously, so that several times Rendrick was hard put to save the *felucca* from being taken aback. Then gradually the wind settled down to blow hard and steady from the east-north-east. There were no clouds, but the air quickly turned colder until they were all shivering. The clouds of spray that swept the open hull wet them through. The strain on the mainsheet increased until Rendrick had to turn it over to Rule, who crouched to windward, his back turned to the spray.

Suddenly Rendrick began to sing, loudly an

tunelessly, but with gusto—in his element, actually enjoying himself, Rule thought grimly. Looking out at the sea to leeward Rule could find little cause for comfort. The brilliant moon, now directly overhead, illuminated a seascape that looked like a plateau of steep, snow-capped mountain ranges. Every wavetop was white with the spindrift torn from it by the gale. The *felucca* was charging through these waves with a curious twisting motion, her broad, almost flat hull working perceptibly as it balanced momentarily on the steep, toppling crests.

"Shallow water," Rendrick yelled, and Rule nodded. There was probably not more than fifteen or twenty feet between them and the seafloor, built up by the silt deposits with which the Nile was perpetually extending its delta. This was why the steep, confused sea had kicked up so quickly, and was not likely to get any calmer.

Daylight came before the moon set, with no change in the weather. Handling the *felucca* in these conditions tested Rendrick's helmsmanship to the limit, but the quick reactions bred by years of fast skiff sailing helped him, and by luffing through the worst gusts he was able to keep the lee gunwale just above the waves. Only occasionally he miscalculated, and then solid water leaped aboard and drenched them all.

Rule did not notice the cold because of his constant tug-of-war with the big sail and the necessity to concentrate on Rendrick's orders, for the sheet had to be eased on almost every wave. As the daylight became clearer he glanced at Jean, whose figure for hours had been a dark, unmoving silhouette, and was immediately anxious about her. She was pale and miserable, seasick, he supposed, and was not succeeding in an attempt to conceal the chattering of her ... Her hair, wet through, hung in lank braids over ... shoulders.

"All right?" he yelled at her.

She nodded and smiled wanly, but the effect was even less reassuring. He leaned towards her and shouted: "We don't need you here. Go forward. Get some sleep."

"I don't know what's the matter with me," she said uncertainly. Her next words were torn away by a mad gust of wind. ". . . isn't the cold. I shouldn't feel like this . . ."

"Off forward," he insisted. "Get going."

She nodded without speaking again and began to move towards the bow.

"She all right?" Rendrick bawled.

"I don't know. Just cold and wet, I think."

"Things'll be better when the sun gets up. That shouldn't be long."

But Jean, who had been standing up in the bow, now began to work her way aft again, bracing herself at every step against the wild tossing. Watching her, Rule thought uneasily that while the wind did not seem to have increased further, the seas were becoming even steeper and more broken, with vicious cross-waves slapping the *felucca* hard amidships. When Jean approached close her voice was so low he couldn't follow her words.

His gaze followed the direction of her pointing finger. Peering through the spray, after a long half minute he made out a low, hard line across the horizon directly over the starboard bow. Once sighted, there was no mistaking what it was. He leaned over and tapped Rendrick on the shoulder.

"What?"

"The beach. Ahead of us and off to the right."

"I thought we had a better offing than that. It's this bloody change in the wind—and it's still veering, I think."

He leaned over and gave the mainsheet a vicious yank, but the *felucca* would not stand being close

101

hauled any further. She balked and plunged her bow deep into a wave. Water sloshed inboard alarmingly.

"So that's enough of that," Rendrick muttered to himself and eased the sheet again. Rule began to bale.

"We'll have to do the best we can," Rendrick said. "If we're where I think we are, near Baltîm, we're rounding the most northerly bit of coast—it bays away again after that towards El Aiyash. Keep an eye on the shore for me and let me know if it looks to be getting closer. It can't be far off if you can see it from this height, only a mile or two."

"Can't we turn?"

Rendrick shook his head and pointed up at the straining sail.

"I wouldn't like our chances. With a crew of six or seven men it'd be bad enough in this weather. To get that sail about we'd have to lower it and then rehoist it to suit the other tack. I just hope it doesn't come to that."

Jean had crept away forward again, and Rule saw her stretched out on the pile of sodden canvas, apparently asleep.

Now, as well as managing the mainsheet, every few minutes he balanced himself against the pull of the rope, rose as erect as he dared, and peered at the low coastline. For half an hour they appeared to be holding their own—certainly the thin, serrated line of sand-dunes didn't seem any closer. Then, with a sinking heart, he watched a dim shape rise above the horizon and rapidly become more clearly defined. It was a blunt cape, probably no more than a low sandbank, but located directly in their path. How far ahead was it? A mile? Two miles? Closer, much closer, he realised with sudden alarm.

"Trouble," he yelled to Rendrick. "Sandbar. Right ahead. Can't miss it on this course."

Rendrick recognised the urgency in his voice and didn't waste time with questions. He brought the *felucca* up into the wind where she hung, the sail flapping and booming. The hull trembled as if it would tear itself apart.

"Come on," he said, and began to scramble forward. The anchor was lying on the floorboards, its rope tangled around the shank. After a terrifying minute they managed to clear the line and lifted the anchor on to the forward deck.

"Now," Rendrick shouted as the *felucca* dived down from the crest of a wave. The anchor shot overboard, the ancient hemp line hissed through the water, then the boat brought up short, with a jerk that shook everything. For a few minutes Rendrick looked down at the straining line, then touched it lightly with his fingers.

"Dragging," he said tersely. "That's to be expected, of course. At least we're moving back slower than we were without it, and it'll keep the bow into the wind and seas. But it does mean we can't just stay here and ride it out. An hour or so, and we'd have drifted back into the surf. We could possibly wait for that, then swim ashore."

"Jean can't swim."

Rendrick's face was expressionless.

"Well," he said, "that makes it easier. We'll have to do what I said, get the sail down and rig it for the other tack. It won't be easy, but at least now we've got her held by the anchor it's more or less possible. That way we can get farther out to sea and give ourselves a bit of room. Once we're out of these shallows she won't jump about so much. It's a miracle, really, that something didn't give way hours ago."

"What exactly do you want me to do?"

"Listen carefully. Because of the crazy way all this is rigged, and the strength of the wind, we'd very likely capsize trying to pass the mainsheet and the sail forward of the mast, as one would normally do. So

103

it's got to come down, then we'll raise it again, on the other side of the mast." He spoke slowly, between the gusts. "Once it's up, I'll get back to the tiller. Here, take this knife. We'd never get that abortion of an anchor up again, so we'll part company with it. When I give you the nod, cut the line. I can pay her off downwind until you get back to the mainsheet. We can make our offing, and still take things easy, once we're safely on the other tack. So don't heave the sheet in too hard. Gradually . . . got that?"

"It'll be gradually all right," Rule said grimly, looking down at his hands, from which square inches of skin seemed to have been flayed by the wet rope.

"Now then."

The sail came down with a run. The boat seemed alive with flapping, sodden canvas and they had to fight for long, despairing minutes to keep the boom from blowing overboard. Then, foot by foot, in a series of cautious movements, they had it ready for hoisting again on the port side of the mast.

"Just one minute's breather," Rendrick said. "With luck, the worst's behind us. If only that bloody sheave in the mast would turn round—but it won't, of course."

"That thing takes some getting up," Rule said. "It was bad enough dry. Now the sail's wet . . ."

"I've been thinking about that. We needn't be too fussy about setting it tidily, so if it sticks halfway we should still be able to sail clear. Also, the wind's going farther round. I reckon it's past east already, moving towards the south. That could be the morning land breeze influence, and if it is, the wind'll go on shifting in our favour."

Rule looked about him. The sun was just rising, and the *felucca*'s seesaw motion seemed a shade easier. The waves were breaking less at the crests.

"It's eased a bit, hasn't it?"

"Possibly. It ought to moderate with sunrise. Just

one thing, it could make all the difference to getting that sail up again if we had Jean's weight on the halyard as well, even though it seems a pity to disturb her."

They looked down at the sleeping girl. Her face was now flushed, the abrasions on it standing out angrily, and she moved restlessly in her sleep.

"We've got just the one chance to do it properly," Rule remarked.

"That's dead right."

"So Jean had better be woken up." He bent down and touched her head.

Then something hideous happened. She moved her head to one side and his fingers caught in a few strands of her hair. These came away in his hand, as though loosened at the scalp. For a few moments Rule looked stupidly at the small lock of fair hair, then he placed his hand on her brow. In spite of the cool air and the dampness of everything her skin burned to his touch. She had a high fever.

"What's the matter?" Rendrick asked, alarmed at Rule's expression.

"She's ill—very ill. I doubt she could even stand up, much less help us with the halyard. Also, we'd better get where we're going bloody quick."

"You know what it is, don't you?"

"Yes. She has radiation sickness."

Rendrick did not speak, but only shook his head slowly.

"It'd be a miracle if it were anything else." Rule went on, "The radiation must have been thick when she went back to the hospital for those women. When she didn't seem sick on the first day I felt more hopeful. The cases that come on later can sometimes be cured—if they're treated the right way. I don't know a lot about it, only what I've read, and according to that, this shouldn't have developed as soon as this."

"What chance has she got?"

"I don't know enough to be sure. I've read that tufts of hair coming out and a high temperature are early symptoms—and look at those cuts on her face. Even the small ones aren't healing well. They're staying open."

"We could be in port in Israel by tonight," Rendrick said. "She could be in hospital in Tel Aviv within hours after that. Come on, we'd beter move. There's no point in mucking about here any longer."

The sail went up easily for the first few feet but once the wind caught it, it began to belly and thrash, jamming the halyard at the sheave. By heaving momentarily as it reached the midpoint of each of its side-to-side flaps, they were able to raise it an inch or two at a time. Two-thirds of the way up, with the boom little beyond horizontal, it stuck again and this time would not budge. The sail bellied grotesquely and thumped the spar as it regularly filled and emptied of wind.

"That's no good," Rendrick yelled. "We'll carry away something if this goes on. It'll have to do. I think I can steer her downwind somehow."

He took half a dozen turns of the halyard around the iron cleat at the foot of the mast.

"Get the knife ready. Cut when I nod," he said.

But some evil Providence inspired the wind to freshen again—a banshee gust that howled down, the dying kick of the storm. The *felucca* heeled far over, then the anchor rope twanged and broke. Rendrick made a dive for the helm, but he was too late. The tiller banged over to its fullest starboard reach, then crashed back again as the rudder swung uselessly to and fro. The *felucca* came fully downwind, then her impetus drove her still farther round. Now the wind took charge completely. Its force exerted directly abeam into the billowing sail, it drove the *felucca* over until water cascaded over the gunwale. Then she turned on her side, the waves smashing over the half-submerged hull in clouds of spray.

Rendrick, leaping for the tiller, had lost his balance. As the boat turned over he was flung straight overboard. That was the last Rule ever saw or heard of him. For a moment he wondered what he could do to help Rendrick, but he was nowhere in sight. Then he saw that Jean was also perilously close to the submerged gunwale, pitched forward on her face. He reached down with one hand and tugged desperately at her. After a few minutes he had turned her over, face upwards, and held her firmly with one hand.

She moved slightly and moaned—at least she was still conscious, but he could not stay long like this, the physical strain would be too great. He thought carefully and looked about, then realised that the safest place remaining was probably the eyes of the bow, under the six feet or so of stout decking. Getting there was another matter, but sheer blind exertion, of a kind of which he had not believed himself capable, achieved it. Jean was no help to him. Delirious, she even tried feebly to struggle free of his grip, but inch by inch, he moved both of their bodies until she was crouched in a sitting position, supported by the bottom and deck-ribs of the hull. By bracing his own feet against the mast-step, he was able to get into a position he could maintain easily, and which would keep both of them relatively secure.

He supposed it wouldn't be long before the *felucca* drifted ashore. She would then begin to break up in the surf. He didn't dare think about what he would do after that.

However, this did not happen. Instead, the wind continued to moderate and shifted farther to the south, so the *felucca* was blown offshore, into deeper water. Her motion eased, and being made entirely of wood, she continued to float relatively high. About noon Rule found he could crawl out along the port gunwale, which was floating a foot or so above the surface. The sun was shining brightly and the wind was now little more than a brisk breeze and considerably warmer. The waves remained high, but their fetch was longer and they no longer broke on the crests.

He clambered up on to the port shroud, looking at the boom, and the tangled sail lying in the water. If he could rid her of this deadweight the *felucca*'s flat-iron shape might allow her to right herself. Most of the individual wires in the shroud seemed thinned by rust, and several had already broken. Methodically he sawed away at the rest, one by one, with the knife. Luckily it was a good blade, and the strands parted easily enough. After perhaps an hour of this, the mast sagged away from the hull.

Nothing happened. He dropped over the weather side, leaning far out and bracing his feet against the keel. Reluctantly the hull began to wallow back, and finally eased on to an even keel. There was a large galvanised bucket amidships, which was tied to the thwart with a length of small rope. An hour's baling with this dried out the bow, where Jean was still lying, and gave the *felucca* some reserves of buoyancy.

He went forward and looked down at Jean. She opened her eyes.

"Michael?"

"Yes? You're awake. How do you feel?"

She smiled wearily. He could see it was a massive effort, and his heart warmed to her.

"What happened?" she asked.

"All sorts of things. You slept through them all. We've lost our mast, unfortunately, but we're still afloat. Someone'll pick us up."

She nodded, too languid to consider this at other than face value.

"I woke up a while ago," she said, and he had to

lean close to hear her faint tones. "You weren't here. I thought you'd gone and left me alone."

"I'd never do that."

She smiled again.

"I'm a bore, being sick like this. I don't know what's the matter with me."

"You've got a chill, that's all. Getting wet through and cold, it's not surprising. Soon we'll have you ashore and in a comfortable bed."

But he had no sooner said these words than she was seized by a paroxysm of dry retching. He held her, unable to help, while this went on for long minutes. At last it passed off and her contorted face eased. She looked very tired.

"Michael?"

"Yes."

"I'm very thirsty. Please, can I have some water?"

"I'll go and get it."

He knew already that the water beaker was not still in the boat. It should have been lashed down, but it wasn't, and it had gone overboard when the *felucca* capsized. There was no water at all, not even a mouthful he could give her to ease her thirst. He waited a few minutes, making a pretence of searching further, until he went back to her, dreading the explanation.

It proved not to be necessary, for delirium had seized her again, and she did not even recognise him, merely lying back, her tongue passing continually over her dry lips. He made her as comfortable as possible, then sat down beside her, swept with a tumult of emotion of a kind he had never before known.

If they were not rescued before nightfall, she would probably die before morning. He considered this thought, turning it over in his mind almost incredulously, and thinking of its implications to himself, for now he knew he wanted this girl

109

desperately, simply wanted to be with her, for all of the future. Anger swept over him like a wave of shock, bitter animal hatred for those people who, in another time and another place, had caused her this harm. This anger had to find physical expression. He clenched his fists and his lips drew apart in the beginnings of a snarl. Then this emotion also passed.

He stood up in the centre of the boat and looked around carefully, studying each small segment of the horizon for long seconds, until his eyes watered. A fiery trail reached out across the water to the *felucca* as the sun dipped towards the horizon.

Nine

The jangle of the telephone woke Blackman early in the morning. It was not yet light, and he turned on the bedside lamp and blinked once or twice before sitting up and reaching out a hand for the instrument. It was so cold he began to shiver at once.

"Who is it?"

"Roberts, from the P.M.'s office," said Clayshot's private secretary. He sounded unnaturally brisk and alert for this hour.

"The P.M. says to tell you the Russians are ready to talk."

"When?"

"As soon as possible, in Moscow. The French are sending M. Dubois separately. They think it's best we don't have everyone on the same plane. The P.M. asks, can you be ready for a seven o'clock take-off? I can have a car at your house at six—that's in a little under an hour. Sorry about the rush—"

"Don't worry," Blackman cut in. "I've been expecting it, and I've kept my bag packed. It's good that something's happening at last."

"I hope it turns out well," Roberts said, but he sounded doubtful.

"You're going?"

"Yes. And so he can be filled in on military aspects, the P.M. has asked Brigadier Simons, from your committee, to be on the flight too. Just one other thing—there's a batch of overnight dispatches in from the Foreign Office—the most important by far is an appreciation from the ambassador in Tel Aviv. The P.M.'s been told the salient facts, but he particularly asked me to see you got copies before we took off, so he can consider the details with you. The packet'll be with the driver of your car, so you'll have a chance to look at them on your way to the plane. I'll see you there."

"Right. Good-bye for now."

Barbara stirred in the bed beside him, yawned and opened her eyes.

"Bermuda?"

"I wish it could be. This damned cold gets right into the marrow of one's bones. Old age creeping on. No, the Moscow journey's on. As usual, now they've decided, the Russians can't make it quick enough." He raised his voice, so she could hear above the whirr of his electric shaver. "But at least for the moment they've come down on the talking, and not the shooting side. When they were saying nothing, and matters just drifted, I couldn't help feeling jittery."

"I could tell you were restless," she complained. "You have that way of rolling over and over, always the same way, so you wrap yourself in the blankets and I'm left with none."

He grinned at her chiding tones.

"Too bad. I could have woken you up and made you talk."

"I shouldn't have minded. Husbands don't talk to their wives half enough about serious things, you know. Anyway, is there any hint about what line the Russians are taking?"

"It seems not, but I can guess. They'll not want to see us just to pass the time of day, or to talk in abstracts. They'll have some very tough deal worked out, they'll already have crossed the Ts and dotted the Is, and our job will be as message-boys—go-

112

betweens with the Americans. Mind you, that's exactly what we expected and, I suppose, even what we hoped for."

"I'll get up and cook you an egg."

"Don't bother. They'll have something on the plane."

She shook her head.

"Food on planes never suits you, especially in this kind of weather. As usual, the forecast is gloomy—fog, sleet and snow, with cold northerlies right across Europe. I always listen when you have to go somewhere."

She was already up, in slippers and a dressing-gown, and was brushing her hair vigorously, as she always did on rising. He glanced at her and reflected that she was still good-looking, which was something to say for a woman of her age at this hour of a winter's morning.

"I prefer to travel when you can come," he remarked.

"I wish I could, but I doubt Mr. Clayshot would approve of camp followers this time."

The car arrived, moving slowly through the fog, at ten to six, while Blackman was still finishing his coffee. He was glad Barbara had made breakfast. Now he felt ready for what was sure to be a hard day.

"You've a packet for me?" he asked the car driver.

The man passed across a large manila envelope with "Most Secret" markings. Blackman opened it, and took out the file inside. The report from Hewitt, the Ambassador in Tel Aviv, must have just come in, since he had been given a carbon straight off the teleprinter, not a typed copy as was usual with less urgent dispatches. It was difficult to follow the smudged letters in the subdued light available in the car, but the material was so obviously important Blackman devoted his whole attention to it on the way to the airfield. This would be large, black headlines in all the world's newspapers later in the day, he thought grimly, as he turned the last page.

There were four or five other single-page flimsies in the file, and he read these quickly. They, too, were significant in quite another direction and would need to be brought to the Prime Minister's attention at this stage.

The car stopped briefly at a checkpoint, then rolled straight on to the tarmac. Blue, green, and orange runway lights loomed up and disappeared in turn through the fog, then he saw the aircraft, one of the government's V.I.P. Concordes, as a dark hawk-like silhouette against the eastern light that was slowly leaching into the sky. This, and an equivalent French official flight, remained the only completed Concordes after United States restriction of the supersonic transport market.

Roberts and Simons were waiting for him at the foot of the gangway, heavily rugged up in coats and gloves. Simons was in uniform.

"Morning Arthur," Blackman greeted him, and grinned pleasantly. "Think the air force'll get us there in one piece?"

Simons returned the smile, a little self-consciously, but attempted no pleasantry in response.

"The P.M.'s already aboard," Roberts, a thin, spare man with anxious eyes, told him. "But he doesn't feel at all well. He has a bout of the 'flu and since he nearly always gets airsick, he's far from cheerful."

"As you'll see," Simons murmured feelingly. "At present he's in a bloody awful state—very bad-tempered. He was using me as a chopping-block for some row he'd had with C.G.S.—also he's been demanding to know, for the last ten minutes, where the hell *you* were. At length I found it warmer waiting out here."

"He's been favouring you with his views on the military?" Blackman asked.

"With a vengeance. I got the impression he felt anyone who was a professional soldier, especially in peacetime, was probably the type who pulled the wings off beetles when he was a little boy."

Blackman and Roberts laughed.

"Don't worry," Roberts said. "He was very insistent on having you along, just the same."

Blackman nodded, and moved up the steps.

"Good morning, Prime Minister," he said formally as he walked up to the front of the aisle.

"It's you, Blackman? And about time, too. Is everyone here? If so, let's be on our way."

"You're feeling off-colour, sir? I'm sorry to hear it."

"Who the hell told you that? Well, it scarcely matters. And don't call me 'sir.' It doesn't come well from senior diplomats."

He glared at Blackman, who met his gaze steadily.

"As a matter of fact," Clayshot said, looking away at last, "I don't feel too marvellous. Got a cold. Then, I find it isn't possible to get a decent undisturbed night's sleep these days. It's the telephone. Haven't you ever thought that no civilised person in their right senses would consider it reasonable to barge into your house at any hour and intrude on you without warning? Yet that's just what they do when they ring up on the blasted telephone.

"Last night, about eleven o'clock, it was Wellesley. He was doing his level best to persuade me into letting him take his toy soldier set out of its box."

Blackman grinned, wondering what the aristocratic Chief of the General Staff, who took himself very seriously indeed, would think of this version of his plea for mobilisation.

"Of course he could well be right," Clayshot

continued petulantly, "but that doesn't make things any easier for me. If there were a major war right now, I suppose I'd go down into history as a sort of Nero, a Prime Minister who fiddled while Britain burned. Wellesley would be left with the comfortable feeling that he, after all, had advised me to do the right thing—if he were still alive, of course. And he could well be. Generals have a remarkable talent for surviving to a ripe old age. Field-marshals do even better."

Blackman shook his head.

"I don't agree with mobilisation, or sabre-rattling of any kind. All the arguments we raised the other day still apply, now more than ever. If the middle powers of the world keep their heads, then there'll be fewer complications for the super-powers to untangle. The very fact that we're sitting here now promises well."

"Shouldn't build too much on that," Clayshot grunted, but Blackman could see he was pleased at such unequivocal support.

"Someone had to come out and give a lead," Blackman went on. "Already there are signs of other people following."

Clayshot looked up inquiringly, but just at that moment the engines whined up to take-off revolutions, and the passengers were obliged to sit silently as the aircraft bumped across and off the wet runway. Although the fog was thinning, it was still impossible to see far past the wingtips, and the city and coastline below remained invisible as they climbed quickly and headed for the French coast.

Clayshot's dislike of air travel was only too manifest during this process.

"I have a theory," he said loudly, "that one only travels on so many aircraft in a lifetime."

However, as the machine levelled off at its cruising

altitude he relaxed, unfastened the seatbelt, and returned his attention to Blackman.

"You were saying?"

The Japanese Prime Minister has made a statement along much the same lines as yours. Whatever happens, they propose to stay neutral. Only an attack on the Japanese mainland itself could provoke them into hostilities."

Clayshot nodded.

"Good for them. They're in the same boat as us, of course, in their crowded little islands, and they're sane enough this time to see their danger. Even though the Hiroshima—Nagasaki business was a long time ago now, the Japanese haven't forgotten what atomic bombing is like.

"It struck me only last night, Blackman, what a large and dangerous factor in the present situation public ignorance of the facts of modern war represents. I've been going around for some years now thinking how impossibly young all the mothers with babies seem these days—mere schoolgirls. Of course they aren't any younger than they've always been—it's just me getting older.

"It's been nearly thirty years since those bombs fell, and a quarter of a century since there's been much serious debate about the effects of nuclear war. Since then a highly-effective soft-pedalling job's been done almost everywhere. Now a generation has entered into its responsibilities which knows next to nothing about what would actually happen if there were a major atomic war. All the nasty stuff, those highly unpleasant facts about what really happened to the people of Hiroshima and Nagasaki—I haven't so much as heard them mentioned for years. People would rather not—"

He groaned as the aircraft bucked through a patch of turbulence, then dropped into an air-pocket.

"All right?" Blackman asked sympathetically.

"Certainly—but that was ahead of schedule. It shouldn't have happened until we were all nursing cups of scalding tea."

Blackman chuckled dutifully at this mild joke.

"On the other hand," he said, reverting to the matters in the Foreign Office file, "there's nothing much yet from most of the Commonwealth. Our High Commissioner in Ottawa comments that the Canadian Government prefers to say nothing official for the time being, but unofficially we're told Canada wants to keep her options very open. There's a bland, short statement from Wellington, supporting you, but with a certain amount of hedging. Delhi, Colombo, Kuala Lumpur, Singapore are all backing you up, with varying degrees of enthusiasm."

"That's to be expected. What about Canberra?"

"You might like to read that one yourself."

He handed the file across to Clayshot, who put on his glasses and read the single-page statement with a deepening frown.

"Curt," he remarked, "and much too forward for such a small nation. Countries of fifteen million don't cut much ice in matters of major world policy, but sometimes they don't realise it. I've never been able to work out why Australian official statements are so often bellicose, when the average Australian seems such a pleasant, unassuming chap. This makes them the only nation so far to commit themselves absolutely to backing the Americans . . . that's how I read the phrase 'whatever happens, Australia will stand by its alliances', don't you?"

"I agree that's how it's bound to be interpreted— but you're not quite right on your first point. South Korea has also said it will support the United States in any contingency."

Clayshot grunted.

"Fine company for the Aussies. Well, it scarcely

matters—as I said they're too small a nation for their government's views to count for much at the moment."

"They feel they owe something to the United States," Blackman remarked.

"Going back to the war with Japan? The Battle of the Coral Sea? Lord, that was thirty years ago! The world's a different place now. Then, there was some sense in expecting another country to look after you. But now, with atomic submarines and I.C.B.M.s everywhere—well, all I can say is that if I were stuck down there with—what is it, twelve thousand miles? —of coastline to defend, I'd be a dedicated neutralist.

"Little boys who play with big boys—especially war games—are bound to be the first to get hurt. You served there for a few years, didn't you?"

"Quite a time ago, during the Menzies era."

"Menzies? Ah yes, the chap that liked cricket so much. Got to be Warden of the Cinque Ports, with all that business about stranded whales. It was he that accustomed the Aussies to their Prime Minister being a sort of father figure. He seemed to mesmerise them, even the intelligent ones. The trouble is they've never got a real dad since."

"There's no doubt they had complete faith in the ability—and willingness—of the Americans to protect them," Blackman said, "and it wasn't the intellectuals and the conservatives so much as the ordinary people in the shops and the factories—even the Labour Party didn't dare question the American alliance."

"Yes, it's a lonely part of the globe they're in." Clayshot's tones were more serious now. "You can see their point of view—that's what brought this on." And he tapped the document on the table before him. "Mind you, I've no doubt the Americans'd be willing enough to protect Australia—after all they've a whale of a lot of money invested there. Yes, they'd be willing enough, but when the chips were really down—say during a major atomic war—what the hell *could* the Americans do if, say, the enemy decided to take a lam at the Australian coastal cities? There's no early warning system, no battery of anti-missile missiles, and no possibility of such a small population being able to afford such things.

"Well, anyway, let's get on with the other business. This stuff in from Tom Hewitt in Tel Aviv—you've seen it?"

"Yes, it's here. It's important."

"That's putting it mildly. You'd better go through it aloud, so we can discuss any points that come up. I think we should have our brigadier in on the talks, too. Turn that chair round on the other side of the table and get him in."

Blackman could see that Clayshot remembered and perhaps regretted his earlier sourness, for he went out of his way to greet Simons and put him at his ease. Simons' ruffled hackles were soon enough smoothed through the exercise of Clayshot's blunt, apparently naïve charm. There was something appealing and boyish about it: I am smiling, so you must like me, Clayshot's manner said. However Blackman recognised it as a deliberate technique and was fascinated how effectively and quickly it worked.

"We'll risk some coffee now," Clayshot said genially, and not until it was brought did he turn to Blackman and say:

"Now, what about it?"

"This was dispatched from Tel Aviv at 1.20 a.m. today. The text reads:

" 'At 1700 hours yesterday, Russian ground forces, under cover of a heavy fighter air curtain, began to move across the Suez Canal into Sinai. These forces are mostly regular infantry of the Soviet Army. They were shifted in by helicopter shuttle from staging points close to the Egyptian bank of the canal into positions between the east bank and a line not more than one mile beyond. It is estimated that by darkness forces totalling at least a full infantry division, with supporting units, were in position.' "

"A division!" Clayshot interrupted. "There must've been helicopters buzzing around like locusts. Just how many men does a Russian division amount to?"

"Around eleven thousand," Simons replied.

"Rather more than just a token force. Go on, please."

"The ambassador continues: 'I was called into consultation by the Israeli Government and undertook to communicate the facts to London as quickly as possible so a reaction could be sought. Meanwhile I advised that so far as I knew the British policy of non-involvement had not altered. Much would depend on whether the Russian forces were advanced farther.

" 'However, I am told officially that the Russians notified the Israeli Government one hour before the operation began that they intended to establish a bridgehead in Sinai which, they claimed, was Arab territory illegally occupied by Israel since the 1967 war. This notification gave the Israeli Government certain important and basic assurances. The major one was that, provided the Russian troop movement was not opposed, it would be restricted to a belt of desert from half to one mile wide along the entire shoreline of the canal from Port Said to Ismailia.

" 'The Israelis referred this development most urgently to Washington, and they were advised to avoid provocative action for the time being, until the situation had been more fully considered in Washington—' "

Clayshot gave a low whistle. Blackman looked up at him in surprise.

"You don't find that particularly significant?" Clayshot asked, looking first at Simons, then at Blackman, without evoking any response.

"It's difficult to make judgements on that kind of thing," Clayshot explained slowly. "But on the spur of the moment, when you read out that sentence, it was my instinct that it might in the end turn out to be ..." his voice trailed away, and he gazed out the window, plainly abstracted.

"Would you have advised the Israelis differently?" Blackman asked.

"Of course not. Yet the real point is, should I have done so if I'd been President of the United States? However, let's proceed."

" 'The Russian move over the canal began at exactly the stated time,' " Blackman continued. " 'It was watched by Israeli forces in fortified positions along what is popularly known as the Barlev Line, and these professionals described the operation as absolutely precise. It would appear the Israeli forces in Sinai were ordered not to interfere, provided the Russians kept within the one mile limit. This was the case—in fact in most places the Russian occupation has been limited to within a few hundred yards of the canal bank.

" 'The above encompasses all I have been told officially. However, other interesting or significant facts to emerge unofficially are these:

" '(i) The force is entirely a Russian one—so far as could be observed no Egyptian troops are involved at all, and the air cover consists entirely of Russian machines—MIG23s and 24s, almost certainly flown by Russian pilots.

" '(ii) We understand that an Israeli army intelligence group, dressed as *fellaheen*, were able to spend some time within sight of the canal. They are said to have reported that Soviet engineers are already blowing up the wreckage of ships sunk in the canal, giving reason to believe that the Russians may now carry out the clearing, dredging and shifting of disabled vessels necessary to bring the Suez Canal back into service.

" '(iii) The occupation was successfully completed without a shot being fired by either side.

" 'Signed 'Hewitt.' ' "

Clayshot, who had been sitting bolt upright, relaxed in his seat and closed his eyes.

"The machine is moving," he said. "This is the beginning of a carefully planned and probably far-reaching Russian operation. When the Russians agreed to meet us, I expected something of the kind. They always prefer to talk against a background of action they have themselves started and which has given them an initiative. The question now is, what comes next? This information is already ten hours old."

Roberts, who had been listening unobtrusively in the background, put in:

"I did lay on the contact you asked for direct from this aircraft to your Foreign Office liaison."

"Good. We shall get the latest information, then. Blackman, would you please talk with your own person in the F.O. Roberts here will take notes and pass on any interim information that might require an immediate reply from me. Also, remind them that anything that might come through from the White House of a policy nature must be relayed on to me without delay. I take it our radio's safe?"

Roberts nodded.

"We're using two circuits, alternating from one to the other, and shifting frequency according to a pre-determined and random computer-controlled pattern. The most an eavesdropper could get would be a single snatch of conversation, and even that would demand a high order of coincidence."

"That sounds adequate. We should get on with it, then." Clayshot leaned towards Simons and began at once to question him about the details of Russian divisional organisation. It was not in his nature to waste time.

"You take shorthand, don't you?" Blackman asked Roberts when the radio circuits had been established. "Good . . . then I'll dictate off what I think the P.M. should know, and you can relay it to him without delay." A short conversation followed over the radio, during which Blackman appeared mainly to be listening. Then he looked up at Roberts and smiled.

"Ready? . . . the Russians have done little more than consolidate their forces in the Sinai strip, and only routine supply movements are continuing. Certainly there's been no attempt to infiltrate the Barlev line, and no shots have been fired.

"The Israelis have been moving all available reinforcements into Sinai. Both sides have been flying high-altitude reconnaissance aircraft since dawn, so they have no secrets from each other where troop and equipment deployment is concerned.

"The Israeli Government has been making repeated and urgent overtures to Moscow in an effort to find out what the Russian intentions are. So far there has been no reply. Indeed, the Israeli ambassador in Moscow has been told not to expect any further information for the time being."

Blackman hesitated for a few moments, as though choosing his words with extra care, while Roberts looked inquiringly at him.

"There are some . . . unusual . . . aspects to the Russian activity in Sinai," Blackman went on. "The Russian force there is considered to be an infantry division, as opposed to an armoured or mechanised division, yet it does not follow the normal organisation of a Soviet infantry division, which is three regiments of riflemen supported by a regiment each of armour and artillery. Artillery support is minimal in this force. The proportion of armour is about normal, but there is an unusually high proportion of auxiliary transport.

"Our defence people consider this significant. If the Soviet division were designed simply to invade Israel, fighting a defensive force as it did so, it would seem to be ill-balanced . . . If it is not so designed, what *is* it there for? We can't yet see an obvious answer to this.

"Suez Canal: There's now no doubt at all that the Russians are planning to get the canal open again as soon as possible. Sunken wrecks have been blown up, and the remains are being dismantled with gas cutting torches and hauled to the banks. Dredges are already working from both entrances to clear silt deposits from the canal floor, and there are concentrations of tugs forming, presumably to move out ships floating in the canal as soon as it becomes navigable again."

He took a deep breath.

"Now the world picture. The situation has deteriorated everywhere, just as might be expected. Russia and the U.S.A. are both establishing their forces on a total war footing. If the worst happens, it'll be mighty sudden—" he stopped abruptly, staring into space, and after a few moments recollected himself. "Sorry, that's about it. Pass it back to the P.M. while I hold the circuit for anything he might want to send."

Within two minutes Clayshot himself was at the radio centre.

"This war talk," he said baldly. "We aren't just being made bunnies of, leaving home at this time?"

Blackman knew what he meant, and shook his head.

"I don't think so. Nothing really unusual or unexpected's been reported. The big powers are jockeying for position and preparing for the worst, as indeed they must do. But I believe the Russians do want to talk seriously with us, and that nothing big will happen until after that."

"That makes sense," Clayshot granted. "No need for us to start running and jumping yet. I was glad to see your F.O. boys puzzled about what the Russians are up to in Sinai. I'm not surprised. There's something going on there we don't know about yet, but I reckon it's for our benefit. If I'm right, it won't be long until we do know."

Ten

At Vandenberg Air Base, north-west of Los Angeles, a major programme of military satellite launchings was by now well advanced. One after another Atlas, Titan 3D, and Thor first-stage rockets rose ponderously from their reinforced concrete and steel launching pads on truncated cones of fiery exhaust. Their fuel exhausted, they hurled on into the stratosphere the slim forty-foot long Agena upper stages that would in their turn locate the MILSATs in orbit. For eight to thirty days these satellites would now circle the earth, ceaselessly monitoring activity below.

Some, placed slightly off the synchronous orbital altitude of 22,300 miles, at which satellite movement exactly matches the earth's rotation speed, ranged slowly back and forth across the Eurasian landmass. Within these metal planets complex optical and electronic devices, able to detect instantaneously the lift-off of land or submarine-launched atomic missiles, reported back continuous negative responses to the MILSAT bases at Guam, Hawaii, New Hampshire, Pine Gap in Australia and on specially-located ships and aircraft.

At much lower altitudes, yet still ninety miles above the earth's surface, photographic satellites took pictures of such clarity that enlargements could isolate a man walking in a city street below. Ringing the earth at about three hundred miles, satellites specialised for ELINT, electronic intelligence, tuned in to radio traffic of the Soviet forces, relaying snatches of information immediately to expert linguists and interpreters who sought patiently to fit them into a coherent pattern. Secret meteorological satellites predicting weather conditions over planned target areas completed this enormously expensive, unprecedented surveillance apparatus which made possible the assembly, in Washington, of an apparently complete picture of Soviet military preparations.

A Soviet MILSAT programme, with equivalent objectives, began on the Siberian missile stations within hours of the first American launchings, so indicating that the Russians were prepared to accept and themselves initiate MILSAT activity, rather than seek to destroy the American satellites with the hunter-killer spacecraft developed from the 1968 Cosmos 248, 249, and 252 launchings.

Ground-based electronic intelligence stations ringing the Communist world tuned their sprawling cobwebs of antennae, capable of picking up and amplifying the feeblest of radio signals from great distances. EC121 radar picket aircraft, modified Super-Constellations with grotesque radomes projecting above and below the fuselages, reluctantly hauled into the air their six ton loads of radios, radarscopes, control panels, computers, and data-processing machinery.

In the Pacific, near Hawaii, and in the Atlantic not far off the Spanish coast, Sea Spider deepsea underwater surveillance systems, powered by nuclear batteries, listened for the propeller beats of submarines, their memory banks ready with information that would enable them to identify instantly the type of boat they heard, its nationality, and whether or not it was atomic-powered. In the United States seven massive radar systems, three on each coast and another in Texas, brought into operation a blanket warning system of the approach of submarine-launched missiles.

While all these devices were furiously, continuously, and tirelessly active, the main actors in this mechanical drama remained dormant. In Russia, dispersed strategically from the Ukraine to the Siberian permafrost region east of Yakutsk, more than a thousand blunt-nosed, one hundred and twenty foot stainless steel rockets stood ready in their steel-lined underground silos. Each of these SS9 intercontinental ballistic missiles was armed with a twenty to twenty-five megaton hydrogen bomb, which it was capable of delivering with precision to a target seven thousand miles away. Nearly two hundred more SS9s had MIRV capability. This permitted them to launch one bomb, attack a second area with an independently-targetable warhead, then proceed to yet a third.

In the United States and at bases throughout the non-Communist world, four hundred B52 strategic bombers were at maximum readiness, and one hundred more were already airborne. Each carried five thermo-nuclear devices in its bomb-bays.

At Whiteman Air Base in Missouri, at Warren Air Base in Wyoming, at Malmstrom, Montana, at Grand Forks, North Dakota, and on other secret sites, arming proceeded of more than one thousand Minuteman 3 and 4 I.C.B.M.s, many of them with MIRV capability.

To protect this aggressive rocketry against enemy I.C.B.M.s, around it were arrayed systems of anti-missile missiles. In Russia 98 of the type codenamed GALOSH by Nato stood ready around Moscow and Leningrad, their radars scanning the skies and computers set to guide them automatically on a collision course with an oncoming hostile I.C.B.M., so the two weapons could meet and destroy each other far up in space. In the United States, in spite of widespread opposition to its immense cost, the first units of the SAFEGUARD system of anti-missile missiles stood complete.

Eight miles off Guam, the Soviet spy-ship *Peleng* was seen to be back on station, relaying intelligence about air and sea movements from the United States B52 and Polaris/Poseidon submarine bases on that island. The big submarines ignored her as they dispersed quietly to their stations in the North Pacific, but she would be an early casualty in the event of outright war.

Simultaneously seventy-eight missile-launching submarines of the Soviet Pacific fleet put to sea, a few from Sakhalin Island and Vladivostok, but the majority from the base at Providence Bay, just across the Bering Sea from Alaska. These boats dispersed to stations from which they could attack every city or town in the western United States with a population above fifty thousand.

The surface naval task forces of both zonal competitors were also cruising towards pre-planned stations, their ships floating equivalents of the automatic computerised weapon systems of the land. In the Atlantic the nuclear-powered aircraft-carrier *Nimitz*, not long completed at a cost of nearly a thousand million dollars, led two other carriers, *Hornet* and *Ticonderoga*, each with three hundred aircraft and anti-aircraft rocket launchers. With them cruised twenty destroyers carrying drone anti-submarine helicopters and the cruisers *St. Paul* and *Oklahoma City*. The operational cost of this task force, and an equivalent one in the Pacific led by the nuclear-powered cruiser *Long Beach*, was upwards of one million dollars a day. *Long Beach*'s radars and associated computer banks gave her, a single vessel, a battle control capability a few short years before possible only to whole fleets, for she had the power to track down and attack hundreds of targets simultaneously over thousands of square miles of sea.

Beyond these enormous major forces were others, less publicised, less likely to be used, but still in existence in spite of the destruction of some of their stocks by both the United States and the Soviets. At secret locations in remote regions, "last-ditch" units stood guard over final weapons that might be used to secure victory in a world ruined but not yet absolutely depopulated.

These included stocks of botulism toxin, a single ounce of which, dispersed efficiently, can take the lives of sixty million people; germs of pneumonic plague which, with its bubonic form, was the Black Death of the middle ages—and of pulmonary anthrax, a fatal lung infection so deadly and easily transmissible that the British island on which it was tested during World War II might not be habitable again for more than a hundred years.

This armoury of covert weapons also included chemicals, like the nitrogen-mustard gases, which sear the skin and linings of the lung and then, months afterwards, kill with bone-marrow disease those few who survive the early symptoms; psycho-agents that induce, for days on end, maniacal behaviour in those exposed to them; and perhaps the most esoteric and refined of all, the nerve-gases, designed to inhibit supply of the enzyme essential to the functioning of the human synaptic process, so inducing at once nervous breakdown at its most intensive, convulsions, heart and lung paralysis, and, within thirty seconds, death.

Eleven

A squadron of MIG23s, in perfect delta formation, exploded out of the eye of the watery sun and took up escort stations above and astern of the British Prime Minister's Concorde as it crossed the frontier into the Soviet Union. They peeled off and disappeared abruptly over the horizon when the Concorde began its landing approach to Moscow.

Dubois' aircraft had been delayed fifteen minutes at take-off and was running late. During the waiting period Clayshot and his party were put into a small, overheated V.I.P. room overlooking the tarmac, where a youthful air force officer, who apparently spoke no more than a few words of halting English, offered them vodka and small, coarse Baltic fish on cracker biscuits.

"Mum's the word, I think," Clayshot said cheerfully to his companions, then smiled broadly at the Russian officer, who looked puzzled, then thoughtful. Twenty minutes passed in silence, broken only by Clayshot's steady crunching of one biscuit after another.

"Not bad, these," he commented at last, then got up to greet Dubois, who had just entered the room. A large black Zim, following a motor-cycle escort of two riders, took them through the sprawling, unfinished-looking suburbs to the centre of Moscow. The car slowed as it crossed the expanse of Red Square, there was a glimpse of the incredible towers of St. Basil's Cathedral, and it passed through a gateway in a wall of pink brick. For reasons no doubt symbolic as well as practical, the meeting was to be in the Kremlin. Finally the car stopped at the porticoed entrance to a modern building, inside which they tramped along echoing corridors to a small conference room, in which the chairs were set to confront one another across an oblong table—an outstanding ugly creation in grey-painted steel.

This was a summit meeting. Blackman was reassured to see Brezhnev, Kosygin, and Grechko all present. Another man he could not place at once he later recognised as the party theoretician Mikhail Suslov.

Suslov was the Russian spokesman. He spoke slowly in his own language, reading from a prepared typescript, while a tall, fair woman next to him translated into English phrase by phrase. There was no translation into French, but this scarcely mattered to Dubois, who spoke perfect English. He wondered if he should protest simply on grounds of protocol, then decided against it. This, after all, was not the U.N.

The preamble to Suslov's speech dealt with the nuclear arms race which, he said, the United States had instigated and in which the Soviets and China, as the "guarantors of freedom," had been forced to compete. The Communist nations, he claimed, had always been reluctant to make nuclear weapons, recognising that sooner or later these must become a grave risk to the future of mankind.

"The U.S.," Suslov went on, "is the only nation so far to have used these weapons. First they attacked the people of Hiroshima and Nagasaki. The world was rightly angered by this barbarous act. So the United States did not again try to use nuclear weapons for its purposes, although its militarists did urge the use of the bomb against the People's Republic during the imperialist dissection of Korea two decades ago.

"Fortunately President Truman averted this atrocity, but the Communist peoples had had their warning. They must now enter 'the arms race,' so a deterrent could be provided to counter possible imperialist nuclear blackmail.

"This so-called nuclear parity has long since been achieved, making it impossible for the U.S. now to use atomic weapons openly and directly. Hence, for many years now it has been its policy to create military *juntas*, men of other nations it has bought with money and the promise of power, to act in the U.S. interest. The list of such places is long indeed. However, I need only cite South Vietnam, South Korea, Thailand, Cambodia among the more blatant examples.

"Also among the U.S. satellites is Israel. There can be no denying this! Now, in these circumstances, another city has been attacked with atom weapons. The bombs that destroyed it were U.S. bombs, although launched by one of its lackeys—"

Clayshot was on his feet, interrupting vigorously.

"I must object! How can we have any reasonable discussion on the basis of such statements? You know as well as I do that the Cairo disaster was an accident, due to the actions of a small, irresponsible group of criminals whom—"

"Order, order now, Mr. Prime Minister!" It was Leonid Brezhnev himself who broke in, speaking slowly in English.

"Come now," he continued. "Please contain yourself! These are things which we have been told. Do you suppose we are so *naif* as to believe everything our American friends tell us?"

"Of course I understand your suspicions," Clayshot said more quietly. "I'm not asking you to take my word that they are baseless—yet I am saying that, if we are to have any sort of useful dialogue, you must for the time being at least assume that the facts as stated are the true ones."

Feeling that now he had their attention, Clayshot went on: "I have spoken with the President of the United States. I must tell you he genuinely and deeply regrets what has happened. He even goes so far as to admit that the supply of atomic field weapons to Israel was a mistake. Yet, he says, it was a genuine mistake, his own. He asks that the poeples of the world should not risk great suffering through an error for which he accepts full responsibility."

The Russians stirred, it seemed uneasily, at these words, and Clayshot paused for a reaction. After a few moments it was again Brezhnev who spoke.

"We, too, do not want world suffering, yet the U.S. must stop believing it can blackmail the rest of the world over the risk of a nuclear war. There is no telling, from our point of view, where that might end."

He paused, then added, with more vigour:

"It is the point of origin of trouble—and terror—that must be removed."

"The President shares that view," Clayshot interposed quickly. "He has asked me to propose that top-level talks begin at once between the major powers, including the People's Republic of China, to decide on action to settle the Middle East dispute permanently."

Brezhnev gave a wintry smile, and shrugged his shoulders.

"We also want such a solution. You suggest talks—well, all I can say is that there have been talks without number going back over too many years, and these have solved nothing. There are certain minimum conditions that we can accept. If you will now be patient, you shall hear them."

He nodded to Suslov, who began reading again from his prepared script:

"There have been many trouble spots, much limited warfare, in the world over the past thirty years, but these things have been contained, de-escalated. There is only one trouble place where the danger has not been contained—the Middle East. Now that nuclear weapons have been used there, the world is in graver peril than at any time in its history.

"It is not just the fate of the Arab and Israeli nations that is in the balance. There is a risk to the whole world that unless drastic steps are taken now, the use of nuclear weapons will continue and increase, within a process of inevitable gradualism.

"To us, there seems no doubt that this could happen. The consequences, being extended over decades, possibly even centuries, of the 'limited' but steadily increasing use of atomic weapons, could be even more tragic than those of a major, all-out nuclear war, which would at least settle matters quickly.

"So, the explosion of the Cairo bombs was not just a small matter, not just something that can be settled by saying 'I am sorry,' and by paying reparations. The building of ten new Cairos, the gift of a thousand dollars to every surviving Egyptian, could not restore the situation as it was last month."

Brezhnev lifted his hand and glanced at Suslov, who now stopped speaking and closed the file before him.

"Excuse me. I shall continue," Brezhnev began, speaking slowly and carefully. "All over the world, for millions of years, perhaps, men died from a variety of terrible diseases. Until recently the deaths from these illnesses were regarded as inevitable, yet now almost all have been conquered by man.

"Yet in order to bring this great blessing there must be pain—small pain perhaps, yet it exists. The little child breaks into tears at the thought of the needle-prick that will bring her protection from a fatal fever. There is a little pain, a brief stiffness of a limb, but at least after that the child is safe. The surgical operation that cuts out the inflamed appendix returns life and health to the individual. The pain, after all, was necessary. One can even say that at such times pain is to the good.

"The atomic arms race in our world is a disease. I do not think we can eliminate it absolutely, yet I remind you, among the means of controlling disease are to get rid of the conditions that breed it, or to remove completely the damaged, diseased, or irritant organism."

He paused.

"What is your specific proposal?" Dubois asked coolly.

"We believe that the existence of the state of Israel has no historic or ethnic justification, and that it is for this very reason it has become a permanent problem to the world. The Jewish state was imposed on neighbours who did not want it, and from whose territory it was made. In being formed, it did injury to the people who formerly lived on that land, and its neighbours.

"Since then the cancer has spread. It's contagion inflamed the whole of the Middle East. Now it threatens every person of this planet."

Brezhnev thumped the table to emphasise each of his last five words, and turned to face Clayshot and Dubois directly. The atmosphere was electric.

"Mr. Prime Minister, M. Foreign Minister, we seek your co-operation, that of the U.S., that of all nations of goodwill, to carry out the peaceful cessation of the state of Israel and the return of its territories to the Arab peoples who are its proper owners."

Clayshot's surprise and dismay were evident in every line of his face, which had turned pale. Dubois looked sour and angry, and muttered something under his breath. Then he said:

"We are to take it, then, that you seriously propose the complete, final dismantling of the Israeli state?"

"Yes."

"How quickly?"

"We suggest one year. The Arab peoples, meeting in conference, have already agreed to this, and have nominated the Soviet Union as their agent, and as a *pro tem* occupying force."

"And that's the purpose of the army you have in Sinai?" Clayshot asked.

"Correct. It is a peace-keeping force."

Clayshot ignored this, saying:

"But what about the people? The Israelis?"

"Our information is that there are many who would prefer the country to become part of the Arab world. It is planned that it should be a separate nation, to be called Amarna, under the trusteeship of the Arab Republic of Egypt and certain other states, with internal self-government, but not possessing for the time being powers of self-government or internal law and order."

He smiled, although his eyes remained hard, and continued:

"The concept is similar to that proposed, in 1968, by some influential Americans, for a state of Sinai nominally independent, but really under Israeli control."

"I can't agree that most Israelis would accept your proposal, or want to stay in such a place," Clayshot said. "Would it be a Communist state?"

"It its people so desired."

"And what of those who did not? Surely there would be reprisals and discrimination against them?"

"There could be guarantees against such things. Of course, if certain Jews were to remain active enemies, or were not inclined to accept the authority of the new state, ordinary law and order measures would have to be taken against them. Those unwilling to accept the new order would be encouraged to leave at any time during the interim period of one year. We suggest an international control commission to oversee this."

"But where would they go?"

Brezhnev shrugged his shoulders.

"Where have Jews always gone? They have no shortage of money, no lack of connections. The Western powers, and especially the United States, should be prepared to provide shipping and accept quotas of Jewish migrants." He smiled. "We might even do so ourselves.

"After all, Israel's population is barely three millions. Even if half of these wanted to leave, they would still be far fewer than crossed the borders of India and Pakistan at their time of independence, and very many fewer than fled from Bangla Desh during the terror.

"And this movement of the Jews would be under immensely more favourable conditions. We suggest that an international agency be established to compensate those who must give up their homes and businesses. We ourselves would be prepared to grant a large loan to the Arab states for this purpose. We do not wish to be harsh, to cause hardship or want. All we want is the historical error corrected. The world can no longer afford it."

Clayshot squared his shoulders, and Blackman could see that his jaw had taken a pugnacious line.

"The fact that we have sought elaboration should not be taken as approval, or even as a concession. The whole idea of arbitrarily dismantling a sovereign state is preposterous. There is not a small state that would not fear, constantly, a similar process. Soon there would only be two, or perhaps three, huge world-zones."

Brezhnev shrugged.

"Perhaps that, too, lies within history," he said thoughtfully, then added, with much more emphasis:

"Let us understand each other completely! What we have told you is not a proposal—it is an ultimatum. It is the very least we are prepared to accept."

Clayshot nodded.

"I can see no prospect of its acceptance."

He glanced at Dubois, and rose to leave, but sat down again upon a wave from Brezhnev, who said:

"Two things remain. First, do you agree that for the time being, all this should remain secret, and known to as few people as possible?"

"I agree," Clayshot said. "I can guarantee our security." Dubois also nodded glumly.

"Good. So to the last point. We must have positive agreement to our plan from the United States, from Europe, from Great Britain, within seventeen days. On the thirtieth of the month, then, by noon Moscow time, we must have your consent."

"And if it is not forthcoming?"

"We may compel you to give it."

"Would you care to indicate the direction of such . . . compulsion?"

"Not at present. It will become obvious. We do not propose to be blackmailed by U.S. threats of a nuclear war."

"But that's an argument either side could use, isn't it?" Clayshot said sharply. There was no reply, and no more this time to delay their rising and departure from the room.

"It's preposterous," Clayshot said angrily, when they were back on the tarmac.

"Indeed," Dubois agreed, "but not, of course, impossible."

"I'm surprised that you think so."

"But why? It is something our thinking has touched upon, in Paris, these last twenty-four hours. The Russians, you know, have that kind of mind. I was a little confused, though, at friend Brezhnev's parables. The reference to surgery is plain enough—Israel is the 'irritant organism.' But what about the little girl, and the painful stab of the immunising needle?"

"Something will come of that," Clayshot responded grimly. "I don't know what, or where, but he didn't say it without reason."

Twelve

Zagrev disliked Port Said from his first sight of its low, depressing skyline, emerging from the barren, treeless strip of partially reclaimed sand between the sea and Manzala Lake.

The town was oppressive and dirty. Even though it was winter and the weather could have been much hotter, the contrast with Moscow was extreme. However, *Novgorod*, moored to fore and aft buoys in the outer harbour, was aloof from the squalor of the port. The one comforting aspect was that he could move aboard into her controlled, air-conditioned atmosphere and begin the job of shaking down her crew. He found that several officers were acquaintances and Commander Rostov, who was responsible for the crew and administration, was an old friend with whom he had lost touch in recent years.

The long closure of the Suez Canal had visibly depressed Port Said, and there was evidence everywhere of unrepaired damage caused by Israeli air attacks. However, the *dhows* and *feluccas* still plied the lake, bringing cotton across from Mataria to the Port Said mills, which were even now undergoing a survey for modernisation and improvement by Soviet advisers. There were Russians everywhere in the street, neatly dressed, serious of mien and always working, while the Egyptians seemed to Zagrev to be untidy, mostly idle, and unduly noisy. He wondered how the partnership of such antagonistic minds would work out, then reflected that it didn't matter after all. The Egyptians were in no position now to choose. They would have to follow Russian orders, which would no doubt be to their good in the long run.

Zagrev was a man of practical mind, and his preoccupation with the relationship between Russian and Egyptian was not merely abstract. As he had feared, he was having trouble with Gamal, and in spite of his tentative efforts to establish a reasonable relationship with his counterpart, they seemed unable to communicate effectively. There was nothing about Gamal of which he could complain specifically. The man was civil enough, but any conversation with him lasting more than a few sentences turned out to be an intolerable strain. What was it about Gamal that made Zagrev feel every time he spoke to him that he must raise his voice and shout as though he were addressing a very deaf man, or one behind a wall of thick glass?

Zagrev's doubts became all the more oppressive after *Novgorod* took on board a party of four more Egyptians, a Lieutenant Maif and three petty officers. They appeared to Zagrev slipshod, shabby in their dress and style, and poorly disciplined. However, they had to be accepted without complaint.

The hours passed without sailing orders, and with them the tension increased. Apart from anything else Zagrev was anxious to get *Novgorod* to sea, where her proper cruising routine could be established, and so he could see for himself how she performed. She was a remarkable machine, even more so than the older atomic boats in which he had served. Her design had a neatness—almost an artistry—that fascinated him. It was still difficult for him to credit that her slim bottle-shaped twin reactors and unobtrusive heat exchangers had the power to drive her four-hundred-foot hull through the water for two hundred thousand miles before the relatively simple operation of replacing her nuclear fuel cores had to be carried out.

There was, however, good cause for these power systems to be engineered with the precision of a fine watch—a reason Zagrev did not much like. Instead of the pressurised water formerly used in atomic power plant heat exchangers *Novgorod* employed the superior qualities of a closed system of a liquid metal—sodium. This operated through yet another heat exchanger to provide the high-pressure steam that drove her turbo-electric main motors, thus ensuring that the steam in the engine-room was not radioactive.

This was a near-perfect system, designed particularly for maximum quietness in operation, so long as everything continued to work properly. However, in the event of a collision, a grounding, or damage in combat, when the seals of the primary heat exchanger might be disturbed, the submarine could not only be disabled but also flooded with dangerously radioactive liquid sodium. It was a fact that he filed away in his mind with the other possible nightmares the commander of a vessel like this must take into account.

Yet in most other respects *Novgorod* gave him little of which to complain. His own accommodation, which was not that originally designed for the commander, was somewhat cramped, but this did not worry him. He had been content to keep on the temporary command quarters his predecessor had used during some electrical rewiring operations—a small cabin that was really part of the sick-bay complex, and which was within the same ventilation system as the rest of the hospital area. The sick-bay could easily spare this cabin since *Novgorod*'s crew were all carefully picked men, psychologically as well as physically resistant to sickness. It was seldom that the main ward was used at all and another small isolation cabin in the sick-bay had never been used since the submarine was commissioned.

Zagrev kept on this cabin for one other reason of overriding importance—that the second element of the permissive action link that fired the submarine's missiles was installed in it, and that rewiring this would restrict the ship's readiness for action unjustifiably in his opinion, even if only for a short time. *Novgorod*'s atomic warheads, each capable of destroying a large city, did not have an "abort" capability built into them. Once her missiles were fired, they could not be stopped or diverted except by an enemy anti-ballistic missile.

As a safety measure then, the missile had to be armed according to a set routine. The process could be commenced only by the captain who kept, always on his own person, a special key that released locks in the warhead compartment of each missile. In order to reach these locks the captain had to climb a short ladder on the outside of each tube, open the third and highest port that gave access to the warhead, place the key in the lock and turn it. This began the arming process, which had to be completed by the starting, adjusting, and setting of the missile's inertial guidance system and computers.

After all this was done, with the missile ready for firing and locked to its target by its automatic navigation systems, the rocket motors would not ignite except when two small black buttons, remote from one another, were both pressed. This constituted the final permissive action link. One button was located in the missile firing room, a small compartment just off the main control room. Only crewmen who showed special passes had access to it, and there was always a guard on the door. The damage control door that gave access to a short passage to Zagrev's cabin and the hospital ward and isolation room beyond was also guarded.

If one button in the permissive action link were depressed a bright red light came on next to the second one, but not until this second button was also pressed would the steam system that drove the missile through the forty feet of water to the surface be activated and the first-stage rocket engine ignite.

Novgorod employed a contact analogue system that visualised for her helmsmen her progress through the water, and so simplified her handling that anyone could learn how to control her within a few hours. The contact analogue system, said by Soviet submariners to have been "borrowed" from the Americans, appeared to the helmsmen as a television image on a screen immediately before them. The picture looked like a broad concrete road stretching ahead across a featureless black plain towards a flat horizon of dull grey. This horizon moved up and down as the boat did. If she turned right, the road curved in that direction to the same extent—if left, the road turned that way. Dark lines, like tar expansion joints, across the "road" moved steadily towards the watcher. The faster the submarine moved, the quicker these lines loomed up, completing a replica of what might be seen by a driver through the windscreen of a moving car.

Zagrev was not a man to enjoy inactivity, even for brief periods. At such times he took to rowing to pass the time. Early on the morning after his arrival in Port Said he shipped his oars, and looked at his command from a hundred feet off with a critical eye. Her pressure hull high out of the water, she appeared cranky and ungainly, as she no doubt would be on the surface, particularly if any sort of a sea were running. Modern though she was, she had residual elements of design that marked her as a Russian submarine. Her conning-tower was not slim and sail-like as in the American boats, but squat and broad, a design factor going back to the days when in

Soviet submarines the conning tower had had to house the tops of the missile tubes.

But what Zagrev saw that concerned him most were the minor but revealing signs of deterioration that any ship soon acquires if she is at anchor for long. There were small but noticeable smudges of rust on the flanks of the hull above the missile compartment, and the deck and conning-tower had been spotted by seabirds. In spite of elaborate anti-fouling measures, he knew that below the waterline a certain amount of marine growth was gathering that could rapidly begin to affect *Novgorod*'s top speed.

When he arrived back on board he found trouble. One of the Russian sailors had lost his wristwatch in suspicious circumstances. It had been on the table by his bunk when he went to the head, but ten minutes later, when he came back, it was gone. Nothing like this had happened before in *Novgorod*, and it was inevitable that the newly arrived Egyptians should be suspected. In Zagrev's absence Rostov had tactlessly taken it into his own hands to suggest to Gamal that his men should be searched. Gamal had refused, exploding into furious rage.

"You must have known he'd take it that way," Zagrev told Rostov tersely. "Surely you thought about that?"

"Only afterwards, comrade," Rostov admitted. "I'm sorry. I can see now I spoke too hastily."

"Well, there's nothing more we can do, except see this whole matter of the watch ends now. Nothing more is to be said or hinted about it, and you can let the crew know that's an order. If there's any more trouble of the same sort, I'm to be told about it, and nothing done in the meantime. But until that happens there are more important considerations."

But were there? Zagrev pondered, after Rostov had gone. Somehow this question of the relationship between the Russians and the Egyptians aboard

Novgorod had to be settled, and in a way that did not leave a residue of bad feeling. This, Zagrev recognised irritably, related directly to the nature of his own contacts with Gamal. It was a matter that had to be settled, and the sooner the better.

"Come ashore and have a drink," he said when he next met Gamal.

"Of course, if you wish . . . but first, I wanted to talk to you about the way my men were insulted—"

"Forget it," Zagrev broke in sharply. "I've spoken to Rostov. He had no right to raise that matter with you, and he's been reprimanded. There is no longer an issue."

Gamal looked at him narrowly, his face flushed, as though he still intended to take it further, then thought better, and shrugged his shoulders.

"I'll come with you," he said, "There's a place on the quay that's not too bad."

It was a waterfront cafe from which, at tables set on the untidy pavement, they could look out at the harbour and its traffic. Zagrev left it to Gamal to order the drink, which turned out to be a coarse Mediterranean red that did little to quench Zagrev's thirst. He sipped the wine sparingly, but Gamal drank steadily and quickly. No sooner had the first two bottles gone than full ones took their place.

After five minutes of silence Gamal said abruptly:

"There must be orders soon. Why do they wait to let us get at the Jews?"

"There's no war yet," Zagrev replied.

"No war? What then would you call a war? Fighting Jews, that's what it has been, what it must always be. Our mistake was we didn't fight well enough, not soon enough, and then—"

He broke off, poured himself another full glass of wine and bolted it in the same movement. His face was beaded with sweat and his eyes glowed with a strange passion.

"You can tell me something," he went on thickly. "You're captain of this nuclear submarine—you should know about such things. You can tell me—when they die, these people, after an atom bomb has gone off—is it quick for them?"

Zagrev shifted uneasily on his chair as he met Gamal's intense stare. He had certainly intended to stir up what was in Gamal's mind, but now the naked revelation of it was unpleasant and mortifying, even though pitiful.

"Yet they were only small, those Cairo bombs," Gamal continued, his voice hoarse. "I'll show you a picture—look!" He drew from his breast pocket a small photograph, neatly covered in clear plastic. Zagrev took it reluctantly, and looked down at the bland-faced, dumpy, dark-haired woman who had been Gamal's wife, and the three little boys who were his sons. Curious, he thought, that these images remain, yet instead of the people themselves, there is only radio-active dust.

"They would have known nothing," Zagrev forced himself so say evenly, although he knew this might well not be true. But what could that matter? "It would have been instantaneous."

"Is it so?" Gamal muttered, his distress plain in his eyes.

"Yes," Zagrev repeated. "I've studied these things. I know." Yet he still felt no emotional response to Gamal's despair. He added: "You're sure they're not among the refugees? Perhaps your family had made a journey out of Cairo at the time?"

Gamal shook his head.

"My wife was a good Moslem. She would not go away from her home, would not take the boys away, without my permission, while I was not there. You see, she was an old-fashioned woman, with the old ideas—to us, those are the right ideas. Yes," he repeated, as though to himself, "the right ideas."

"You're suffering from a delayed shock," Zagrev said quietly. "It is a severe mental injury, medically speaking, for a man to lose everything as you have done. You must recognise this, and act accordingly. I know what it's like.

"I hadn't told you, had I, that I'm quite alone? I was away, fighting on the western front, when Leningrad was under seige. For nine hundred days they attacked the city and it never fell, but the damage was very great and the sufferings of the people terrible. Thousands were killed on one night in the winter of 1943, when the Germans air-bombed from dusk until nearly dawn the next day. It was three months before I knew my wife and daughter died that night. I have no one else."

Gamal looked at him with greater interest.

"Didn't that make you want to kill a lot of Germans?"

"For a time—yes. As for now, I don't know. I hadn't thought of it for a long time."

"I would like to kill some Jews," Gamal said thoughtfully. His hand was shaking as he poured the rest of the wine into his glass, so the red liquid slopped over and immediately soaked into the sun-cracked wooden surface of the table, leaving a dull stain. "Kill them slowly. Operate slowly, with a knife. A red-hot needle. Kill a Jew-girl."

Zagrev watched him narrowly, unable to quell a rise in his gorge at the perversity of Gamal's anger. The words themselves, the images they brought to mind, were bad enough, but were nothing compared with the viciousness so plainly apparent on the man's face. The Arabs, Zagrev thought suddenly, were a people of blood-feuds. For them one killing was not enough. There must be more, then more again. The vast majority of the human race asked for their troubles, he reflected bitterly.

There was wine on the table again, and at once

Gamal fell on it, drinking with a passion that could only be described as ferocious, as though he wanted release as quickly as possible from the frenzy of revenge that possessed him. From time to time he mumbled an incoherent phrase, but did not offer to refill Zagrev's glass and seemed no longer aware of his presence.

Then he staggered to his feet, weaving a perilous path to the fly-infested latrine enclosure standing by the cafe's boundary fence with its neighbour. His return journey was even shakier, but he reached his chair in time to collapse into it, his face down on his hands. There would be no more drinking, for the time being, anyway. Gamal was dead to the world.

Zagrev wondered how he would get Gamal back to the submarine, but was spared consideration of this point by the appearance of *Novgorod*'s fast motor-boat, her crisp wake cutting a neat line across the scummy surface of the harbour. Within five minutes she had berthed, and Rostov appeared.

"What is it?" Zagrev asked, more sharply than usual.

"Orders, comrade," Rostov said. "Urgent. From Moscow."

"That's as well. We've been in this hole long enough. Now, Rostov, see to Commander Gamal."

Rostov was astonished.

"Your pardon, comrade?"

"You heard me. Get a couple of men and help him back to the boat. And don't talk about what you see—tell the boat's crew that, too."

Thirteen

The orders required *Novgorod* to be on station, at a position in the region Zagrev had anticipated, not later than noon Moscow time on the twenty-ninth of the month. At any time until then he was to expect further instructions. These could reach *Novgorod* even while she was submerged, through the very low frequency radio equipment that linked Moscow with the missile submarines at sea.

So important and vulnerable were these huge antenna arrays that silence from them for more than a certain period brought into operation a plan which obliged all Russian missile submarines at sea to fire on targets in the United States. Failure of the VLF signals could only mean that the transmitters had been destroyed by surprise enemy action. Twice every day all submarines at sea received routine checking signals. If forty-eight hours passed and no signals came, the submarines were required to surface and attempt to communicate on conventional radio frequencies. If the homeland still remained silent, the submarines must then take independent retaliatory action against targets determined by the individual ship's position at that time.

Even at *Novgorod*'s impressive cruising speeds, there was no time to be lost if she were to reach station on time. Zagrev had been back on board less than half an hour when her nine-foot propellers began to turn, raising vortices of mud from the harbour bottom. The submarine proceeded at five knots into the Mediterranean, and turned west. It was as well the northerly gale of the previous night had blown itself out, for his orders required him to proceed on the surface until *Novgorod* had cleared the Straits of Gibraltar. Even then, in spite of the discomforts and hazards of surface cruising in the open Atlantic, she was to continue it at the best speed possible, in a north-west direction.

It was known that *Novgorod*'s movements would be noted and reported on by the invisible presence of at least one American military satellite, and for this reason an initial appearance was to be given that she was joining K task force off the Irish coast. In order to lend conviction to this feint, three other Russian missile submarines had been ordered from the Mediterranean the previous day, and had actually joined K force. The British would now hear that *Novgorod* was also proceeding to a rendezvous with K force and, knowing that she was one of the most heavily-armed Russian submarines, would feel no happier for this. So the ruse would serve a double purpose.

However, its primary reason was to allow *Novgorod* to avoid pursuit. Granted reasonable discretion in their handling, only a few years earlier nuclear missile submarines of both zones could be considered immune to attack or interception by any other weapons system. This invulnerability could now be maintained only if the missile submarine could by deception or sheer luck eliminate the possibility of her observation by the one enemy that could now overhaul and eventually destroy her, just as safely and surely as a battleship had once been able to sink a cruiser.

This enemy was the specialised nuclear attack submarine, designed from the drawing-board as a hunter and killer of missile submarines. The American Narwhal attack boats, the first of which was completed in 1970, had the most refined sonar search gear in existence and, with submerged speeds well above forty knots, could easily outrun the more heavily-laden missile submarines. Hence the attack submarine, once in contact with her quarry, could if necessary follow it around the world, and close for the kill at any time.

Thus the important consideration for a missile submarine was to avoid the initial sonar contact from the hunter. There was no evidence that the Americans yet had attack submarines in the vicinity, but if *Novgorod* were to survive to carry out her mission, the possibility had to be taken seriously into account. Zagrev was uneasily aware that there was no way of being really sure. An American attack submarine could shadow *Novgorod* for days—even weeks—and never betray her presence until the second when all ended in a blinding explosion.

Alone in his cabin, thinking about these facts, Zagrev concluded that *Novgorod*'s departure from the Mediterranean must inevitably appear logical and consistent to American planners. In the case of war a missile submarine caught inside such confined waters as the Mediterranean would be doomed. Her best place would be either inside the defensive net of such a fleet as K force, or concealed submerged in some remote part of the great oceans of the world.

He was annoyed when a knock on his cabin door intruded on these thoughts.

"Who is it?"

"Rostov."

"I asked not to be disturbed."

"I'm sorry, comrade. It's an urgent matter."

"You'd better come on in, then."

He glared at Rostov as he entered, but the commander responded with a tight-lipped smile. He said nothing, but crossed to Zagrev's desk and put down on it three automatic pistols and six fully

154

loaded ammunition clips. Zagrev picked one up and looked at it distastefully. They were soft-nosed heavy calibre bullets, inaccurate at any distance but murderous at close range.

"Where did these come from?"

"Nurayev—one of the stewards—accidentally knocked over a clothing locker while he was cleaning the cabin our friends the Egyptian petty officers are using. The locker door came open, and one of these guns fell out. Nurayev brought the matter to me, and I then looked inside the locker. I found the two other weapons and the clips under a pile of clothing. Although you'd said to avoid any trouble with the Egyptians, I thought this time—"

"And correctly," Zagrev broke in. "Of course I had to know about this."

Neither man needed to stress the seriousness with which the matter must be regarded. In contrast with *Novgorod*'s power to kill millions of people, her crew did not carry side-arms, except under special and unusual circumstances. There was no normal expectation of having to fight enemies aboard the submarine herself.

Zagrev took up one of the pistols, holding it carefully by the barrel, and squinted down at it.

"Gamal's still out to it, I suppose."

Rostov shrugged his shoulders in a gesture of distaste.

"I imagine so."

"Wake him up then, with a bucket of water if necessary. Get him here at once."

Zagrev continued what seemed a casual inspection of one of the pistols, meanwhile whistling softly and tunelessly, until the door opened again. Gamal came in, looking tired, pale, and tousled.

"My regrets for disturbing you," Zagrev said with deceptive softness. "Thanks, Commander Rostov—please shut the door as you go."

He watched Gamal's gaze drop to the surface of the desk as he sat down. Gamal could not inhibit a start of surprise when he saw the weapons.

"You recognise them, I see," Zagrev said coldly.

Gamal sat back in his chair, staring blankly. Zagrev wondered what was passing through his mind. After twenty seconds Gamal said calmly enough: "They're issue pistols of the type used by my men."

"I knew nothing about them having side-arms. They weren't wearing them when they came aboard. How is it they were found concealed?"

"You've been searching our cabins, then?"

"It seems that might have been prudent, but as it happens they were found by accident. I ask you again, why were they concealed?"

Gamal looked sulky, then shrugged his shoulders.

"It's nothing. My men thought you'd take their arms from them if you knew about them. They wanted to keep them. It seemed easiest not to wear them."

Zagrev would have suspected attempts at evasion or a more plausible excuse. As it was Gamal's explanation was simple, and had the ring of truth. It was just what he would have expected from the Egyptians.

"However," Gamal went on, "I am sorry—deeply sorry—they've been found in this way. I know you have regulations on security, but after all, it has been a misunderstanding. You surely do not think—"

Zagrev lifted his hand.

"I think nothing," he interrupted sharply. "Now look here—it is essential that we work together in harmony, and without concealment. We must at least appear to speak with one voice, especially where the men are concerned. If we have differences, let's air them in private. And there must be no more of this kind of thing."

Gamal looked crestfallen.

"I've been at fault," he admitted. "I'll speak to my men. I will see that matters improve."

On impulse he dropped his hand to the holster on his uniform belt, drew his own pistol, then dropped it on to the desk.

"You'll wish to have this one, too."

Zagrev hesitated. Strictly speaking, that should be the case, but Gamal was, after all, an officer and his counterpart, and the fact that his pistol had been taken from him was bound to be noticed. Gamal would resent this, and feel he had lost face. Inevitably this would become a further cause of friction.

"That's not necessary," Zagrev said at last. "I'll keep these three guns in my safe, also the clips. As for this—" and he handed Gamal's pistol back to him. Gamal carefully replaced it in its holster.

"Thank you. I'm pleased you have confidence in me, indeed it is so. Also, I must apologise . . . I would like to apologise, for my drunkenness. I behaved like . . . like a pig."

Zagrev found it difficult to suppress a grin at this word, which, for a Moslem, was extreme self-accusation.

"You're going through a difficult time," he answered carefully. "Drinking and talking in that way probably did you good. Let's look at it that way, and forget it now."

While *Novgorod* was cruising surfaced the lookout position on the conning-tower was manned as a matter of routine. That afternoon a young sailor from the Ukraine, Basil Selnov, was posted there. It was a good opportunity to bask in the westering sun, which he found much more pleasant than the infra-red lamps in *Novgorod*'s gymnasium. It made him feel indolent, and prompted pleasant speculation about a girl he fancied in Kiev, whom he had been too shy to approach, but whom he now handled most boldly in his daydream.

Because of this Selnov did not see the object floating on the sea until the submarine was quite close to it. It was now almost sundown. He looked more carefully and saw something move. A hand came up and waved in the direction of the submarine. Selnov reported it at once, and, while he waited, looked curiously at the dismasted boat. Minutes later came the sound of feet on the steel rungs of the ladder approaching the tiny lookout as Zagrev and Gamal came up.

"Floating over there, Comrade Captain," Selnov said. "It's hard to see just now because it's so close to the sunset. Look just north of the sun."

"Yes, I've got it. Give me your glasses." He took the binoculars and focussed them. *Novgorod*'s movement had now shifted the relative position of the wreck farther north of the setting sun, and it had become easier to see.

"A small craft, lying low in the water," Zagrev remarked. "Something's in the water close to it, overboard—the mast and sail, I suppose. But I can't see any signs of life."

"There was a man aboard before," Selnov said.

"You're sure?"

"I'm positive, comrade. He was there until just before you came. He must be lying down now."

"Please take a look, Commander Gamal," Zagrev said formally, and passed over the binoculars.

"It's a Nile river *felucca*," Gamal said after a few minutes' inspection. "Some fool has brought her out into the open sea. That northerly last night must have got him into trouble."

"He'll be picked up, of course," Zagrev said.

Gamal handed back the binoculars, and shook his head.

"Perhaps, but I think not. See, the wind is still offshore. The *felucca* will drift farther and farther out to sea. Already she is out of the path of the coastwise traffic."

Zagrev considered this unwelcome information.

"I don't like just to leave a man like that," he grumbled, "but our orders are to stay at sea and not stop without good reason—also there are regulations about unauthorised people on board our nuclear boats . . ."

His voice trailed off. Gamal and Selnov avoided his eye and said nothing. They continued to watch as *Novgorod* began to leave the *felucca* astern.

"We'll go down," Zagrev said harshly, and was just turning when Selnov, his voice expressionless, said: "The man's there now, Comrade Captain. See, he's waving."

In spite of himself, Zagrev looked back. The figure of the man was rapidly growing smaller, but they could make out his hand moving.

"Poor devil," Gamal said quietly. "He'll be a fisherman or a small merchant."

Zagrev recollected his own secret dread, that of many a sailor, that some day he might be sitting in a disabled boat far from land, and watch a ship loom up, come closer, then sail on apparently without seeing him. He could sense the bitterness and despair of the man in the *felucca*, and his hands tightened on the handrail of the lookout point. The sun was already down. Soon it would be night. Zagrev turned abruptly, and took up the intercom phone to the control room.

"Commander Rostov, please . . . Rostov? Good. Heave to, swing out the motorboat, and take a look at a small boat just astern—a native craft, disabled. There's at least one man aboard . . . yes, I know, I've thought about all that. The fact is there's nothing secret about our movements at the moment, and we can put him ashore in the motorboat as we pass Alex tomorrow."

Novgorod slowed rapidly as the propellers went into reverse pitch and within minutes was wallowing lazily on the waves, now long and oily. The electric davits were swung out from the watertight hold that housed the motorboat, and she was soon in the water. They watched her start up and race back to the *felucca*. At this distance it was difficult to see what was happening, but the Russians appeared to be lifting an inert figure across into *Novgorod*'s boat.

"A dead man," Gamal said.

"I think not. They're not such fools as to bring back a corpse. It'll be someone injured, and that's a complication of the sort I don't want."

They waited silently on deck until the motorboat was alongside again, and Rostov's face turned up towards them.

"One man, in not such bad condition, also a woman," he said. "The woman is very sick, with a high fever—also, these people are not Egyptians."

"Get them on board then, and stow the boat," Zagrev said. "The woman'd better go straight to the sick-bay, and Comrade Solyikin can see to her. If the man's not too exhausted, bring him to me in my cabin . . . Come, Gamal, this is something we must get to the bottom of."

"You'd better sit down," he said in Russian five minutes later, after a single glance at Michael Rule. Rule was swaying slightly on his feet, and plainly exhausted. He stared back at Zagrev uncomprehendingly.

"English. Anglais," he volunteered, his voice low and hoarse.

Zagrev nodded, and spoke again, this time in English.

"So. Well, first you had better sit. Now. Who are

160

you? Where are you from? Why were you aboard that boat?"

"An English tourist. The woman with me is a doctor—she's Australian. We were in Cairo, but we escaped, by road, to Alex. We were too late. The last planes had gone. We knew if we reported to the authorities, we'd be interned. So we bought the *felucca* . . . tried to sail it to Israel. Last night . . . the wind . . . we capsized. . . ."

"Not only that. She has a fever."

"Our doctor is investigating. Soon he'll report to me here. And you . . . you need food? Water?"

"Thank you for picking us up . . . I know . . . a great nuisance. We had no water, you see." Rule involuntarily ran his tongue over his dry lips.

Zagrev rose, filled a plastic beaker from the refrigerated water cooler, and handed it to Rule. A knock came at the open door, and Zagrev looked up. It was Lieutenant Solyikin, *Novgorod*'s doctor.

"Come in."

Solyikin looked worried, yet at the same time curiously elated.

"This woman is extremely ill, Comrade Captain," he said at once. "I'm not absolutely sure what's wrong with her, but I'm very nearly so. There are symptoms consistent with atomic radiation sickness. If that is so, she will almost certainly die. We may be able to treat her—from our own point of view it would be invaluable, experimentally, proving techniques that are now merely theory . . ."

"Isn't that risky?" Zagrev asked.

"Yes, but until they're tried, we shall never know . . . and if she is not treated she will certainly die. If she is moved again, or there is any delay in the necessary operation, it will be fatal. The chance will pass tonight . . . within a few hours."

Zagrev looked at him steadily for a few moments, then turned to Rule.

"You don't understand Russian?"

"No."

"Solyikin reports that she is very ill, he believes with radiation sickness. You said, didn't you, that you were both in Cairo? So, it is easy to explain. And for yourself . . . are you feeling any symptoms . . . weakness, nausea, dizziness?"

Rule shook his head.

"She was heavily exposed to radiation, but I was on the outskirts of Cairo. I don't think I have any bad effects."

"None that you know of. They may be yet to come. You'd better go along with Solyikin and let him check you over. Then you should have some food and sleep for a while."

He began to talk with Solyikin again, in Russian. This continued for five or six minutes, then Solyikin beckoned to Rule, and turned to go.

"Can't you put us ashore?" Rule asked. "If Dr. Marsden doesn't get proper treatment, in a hospital, she's certain to die. What does your doctor say to that?"

Zagrev looked up, plainly annoyed.

"I told you Solyikin said that if she were moved again, it would be fatal. Also, if she is to be saved, he must operate tonight. I have authorised him to do that. Come now, even if your friend lived until tomorrow, how do you think she would be treated if we put you ashore? Every hospital, permanent and temporary, in Alexandria is already over-burdened with victims of radiation sickness. But you're a tourist, you say? What d'you do when you're not a tourist?"

"I used to be an engineer—a professional engineer."

"So. And what conclusion do you come to about the ship you are in?"

"She's very big for a submarine . . . she's nuclear-powered, of course?"

"Yes. She is *Novgorod*, one of the largest and most powerful submarines of the Soviet Navy. So, if you think about that for a few moments, you will understand that there are not many places in the world better-equipped to deal with the effects of radiation. It is something that can happen here at any time—to one, two, perhaps twenty men at once. Dr. Solyikin is part of our crew because he is one of the five best-qualified specialists in nuclear medicine in the Soviet Union."

Fourteen

"We can talk," Solyikin, a tall, bear-like man, said with a smile as they entered the sick-bay. "My English is not so good, but I can understand better than I talk—if you speak not too quickly."

"How ill is she. Is there really much you can do?"

For answer Solyikin drew back a curtain and looked down at Jean, who was sleeping. His affable expression turned grim.

"It has the devil in it, that radiation," he said softly. "When it attacks a person, its damage goes deep—yes, deep, as deep as it can go, to the marrow of the bones. There, in what is normally the most protected place, nature has located the delicate machinery that controls and replaces the blood. After a certain dosage of radiation, that machinery runs wild. It is out of control.

"Yes, it is as Comrade Zagrev has said . . . she is very sick. But I have given sedation. For the moment, she needs no more attention."

He turned aside and asked: "Now you. You feel good? . . . bad . . . ?"

"Only tired and hungry. Otherwise normal."

"Any wounds? Show me—even little ones."

He looked carefully at the small cut Rule had got from flying glass in his Cairo flat, and grunted.

"It heals good. Not to worry there. Now, this—" and he thrust a thermometer at Rule's face.

"Normal," Solyikin said after a minute had passed.

"You have had any vomiting . . . diarrhoea . . . ? No? That is good. You continue very lucky. Nothing of the radiation worries for you, my friend, not yet, so probably not at all and if then, not so serious. Your friend the lady doctor is not so lucky. A good friend, no? Sweetheart?"

Rule nodded.

Solyikin's eyes narrowed.

"Is a bad case—worse than I have seen for many years . . . what I now must try is mostly theory. Not enough is known about bad radiation effects. Some years ago everyone said 'blood transfusions,' but no, in so bad a case as this the wild cells in the bone marrow can attack and destroy the new blood. Your friend's blood cell count is very low now—so bad she must certainly die if nothing is done. There is only one chance, so we must take it. I will tell you.

"Some years ago there was an accident at a reactor in Yugoslavia. Four men got almost lethal doses of gamma and neutron radiation. They were taken to Paris and given transfusions of human bone marrow. They lived. Yet even this is known to be dangerous. To transfuse with bone marrow is like an organ transplant. Antibodies are set up. The new bone marrow has to protect itself against the irradiated host. So the sick man is saved from death by radiation sickness, only to find that months later this new syndrome, this wasting sickness, comes on. It is generally fatal."

"So that could happen to Jean?"

Solyikin frowned.

"I will try to avoid it—there is still another way. So, she is a doctor—her training is too valuable to lose. There are not enough good doctors. What did she do in Cairo?"

"She worked in a small hospital run for the poor people by the Quakers."

"Quakers? Quakers?"

"A small religious group, who do not believe in violence and war."

"Tell me, what did Doctor Jean do when the bombs exploded in Cairo?" Solyikin asked.

"She was at home, at her flat, probably a safe distance away. If she'd driven out of the city immediately, she might not have been affected. She went back to the hospital, to the dangerous area, to help the patients. I met her on the way, when she was driving an ambulance to Alexandria, with six women patients in it."

"What happened to the women?"

"They all died."

The memory of what the dead women had looked like flooded back into his mind in all its detail. The thought struck him like a physical blow that the same deadly, eerie processes were already at work in Jean's body. The room seemed to reel about him, and he felt Solyikin's hands on his shoulders, guiding him to a chair.

"Mild shock is setting in. Do not worry. Is natural."

Solyikin's voice seemed to be coming from a great distance.

"Drink," he commanded.

The neat spirit in the glass seared Rule's throat, but restored his capacity for simple physical control over himself.

"Better?" Solyikin asked.

"Yes."

"Is good. Now I will explain. Captain Zagrev has given me permission to operate, to use some of our refrigerated stocks of bone marrow plasma. We are equipped to save those exposed to high radiation if possible. You will ask, what is the good of transfusing this plasma if antibodies are set up? It is here that I plan to use a technique that is experimental.

"In this operation, I will use a high-power X-ray

machine—gamma radiation, it is just the same as X-ray—to irradiate her whole body with what would normally be a lethal dose. What does this do? It destroys all of the bone marrow cells, including the diseased ones, which have been damaged by the radiation of the bomb. Left so, of course she would soon die. But it is at this point that we transfuse the new cells.

"If all goes well they will multiply and move through her bone marrow system. Also, since the existing cells have already been destroyed by the X radiation of our machine, no antibodies should later be set up."

"So there is a good chance?"

"Not enough is known about it. Probably a good chance, yet there is one more factor, of luck. The bone marrow we give her must happen to be a compatible type. Probably it will be, but there is still that risk in this type of operation."

"When will you do it?"

"As soon as possible. My assistant is preparing the X irradiator now. Every hour is important. When did she first become sick?"

"It was very plain by early this morning. She didn't complain the day before, but thinking back I can see that she probably felt unwell then."

"And the exposure was only on Saturday. It is strange that the sickness should onset so soon, when it was not immediate."

"When will you know if the operation's succeeded?"

"If she lives through the night at least the transfusion will be a success. Then we must wait and see. Her general health will indicate."

A steward came into the room with a tray.

"Food for you," Solyikin said, and looked on benignly as Rule disposed of the meal.

"Much better, eh? Now, this also for you . . ." and

before Rule could move or protest he deftly lanced his arm with a sedative needle, and drove the plunger home.

"So, while I am busy you can sleep. Have the sweet dream," he added sardonically and these words, sounding as though echoing down a long tunnel, were Rule's last confused impression.

When Rule emerged into the dreamlike state between sleep and waking, he was at first unable to orientate himself. The strong sedative had left a half-drugged feeling, a disinclination to move or to face reality. He opened his eyes, expecting to see the large window, looking out on to a courtyard, of his Cairo flat, but it was of course not there. Instead his gaze fell on a white-painted wall, above it a low ceiling across which ran the rectangular ducting of *Novgorod*'s air-conditioning system and a bundle of colour-coded electrical cable as thick as a man's arm. This alien room was not still, but in constant restless movement, the uncomfortable pitch and roll conveyed to the submarine's hull by the Atlantic swell.

Reality seeped gradually back into his consciousness, and he shook his head once or twice and got up, struggling to keep his footing in the uneasy motion. The room was full of small sounds—creaks, squeaks, and rattles—as the hull worked and flexed in the waves.

Through the door-curtain was the main sick-bay ward. The screen in front of Jean's bed was drawn back and he saw her at once, a quiet, remote figure neatly covered by a sheet and a single blanket. Perhaps it was the last mists of the sedative, perhaps the silent, motionless figures of the tableau before him, that gave it a quality of unreality.

Zagrev was in the room, looking down at Jean. As he heard Rule's footsteps Zagrev glanced up, his expression still bearing the traces of strong emotion. Rule thought he saw both pain and affection in it. Then the captain's face hardened, he turned away, and left the room without speaking.

As Rule moved towards Jean, Solyikin's voice came from behind him.

"Don't touch her!"

"You've done the operation?"

"Yes. Thirteen hours ago, while you slept."

"She's . . . ?"

"Asleep. Take care you don't wake her. She must sleep as long as possible. There is some sedation—that will help. Now she must be kept undisturbed, away from sources of infection. Later, if the cell count remains low, another transfusion might be needed."

Solyikin's voice was curt, almost brusque, and his manner much more formal. The change of attitude was obvious to Rule, and he wondered uneasily what had caused it.

"The captain now wishes to talk with you again," Solyikin remarked.

"He was here a few minutes ago, and he said nothing to me himself."

"You are to go to his cabin. Although it is very close, be careful to stay in front of the men who will escort you. Do not think to go any place in the ship except where you are told. You understand? If you do not obey, it could be a serious matter."

The two ratings who escorted Rule along the few feet of passageway were tall, heavy, and capable of holding their own anywhere, Rule thought. They were taking no chances with him. The sailors allowed Rule to precede them into the captain's cabin, but he noticed the door stayed open and they waited, in clear view, just outside.

Zagrev, in white tropical uniform, was sitting behind a metal, plastic-topped desk while just off to his right, also seated, was the swarthy figure of the

Egyptian officer Rule had noticed the previous evening. Gamal made no apparent response to Rule's entry other than to regard him steadily with dark, angry eyes. Whatever else happened here, Rule thought, he could expect little help or sympathy from the Egyptian.

The surface of Zagrev's desk was tidy, almost empty. A small framed photograph stood on it, of Jean Marsden. Then Rule told himself this was impossible, for the picture was of a child, a schoolgirl.

"My daughter," Zagrev said quietly, noticing Rule's surprise. "She is not alive now. Like my wife, she died during the siege of Leningrad."

"I'm sorry."

"It was a long time ago, Mr. Rule," Zagrev responded formally.

"For a moment I thought—"

". . . a remarkable resemblance," Zagrev broke in. A shadow passed over his face and disappeared again. "I am very conscious of it. Also, my daughter was very like her mother—" He recollected himself and added briskly: "It is strange what coincidence can do, Mr. Rule."

Rule's uneasiness increased at this repetition of his name, for he remembered that when called on to identify himself the previous evening, he had not mentioned it.

"Can you tell me how long we shall need to stay with you, and where you can land us?" he asked, in an effort to keep the initiative, even briefly.

"I can't tell you either thing," Zagrev said curtly. "It is a matter for higher authority. Perhaps in the end it will be decided in Russia."

"So we are bound for Russia?"

"I did not say that. Now—to establish some facts—you're a tourist, Mr. Rule, who happened to be in Cairo?"

"That was what I said."

"And it was a lie!" Gamal was on his feet, and his voice was raised and harsh. He walked slowly up to Rule and then, in an unexpected abrupt movement, hit him heavily on the right cheek with his open hand. Rule felt the sting of the blow. At first came blank amazement, then a swift surge of rage. His own hand rose to strike back, but he heard a movement behind him and realised that resistance could only limit his freedom to no useful purpose. He breathed in deeply and swallowed his anger.

"That wasn't necessary," he said mildly.

"Only the truth is necessary," Gamal said. "And the truth is that you're a spy—a British spy, aren't you? Admit it . . . see, we know about you. But also we want to know why you're here, what you want, who sent you. And quickly," he said, with a final, abrupt bellow.

Rule, looking at Gamal, saw his eyes narrow and knew the Egyptian was going to hit him again. There was no time to dodge before Gamal struck out, this time putting all his weight behind his clenched right fist. At the same time *Novgorod* rolled heavily, so that Rule fell full-length, hitting the back of his head against the doorjamb. Zagrev watched narrowly, but said nothing and made no attempt to interfere.

Rule clambered to his feet, taking his time about it, and once more faced his inquisitors. He tried to force his brain to consider what was happening dispassionately, reasonably. How did they know who he was? Was there really any purpose in trying to conceal his identity, he wondered, as he saw Gamal lift his hand again? This time, Zagrev spoke.

"Come now, Mr. Rule—surely this is all a little pointless? You must know that we need to have the facts about you. It is our duty. Already we know enough to be absolutely sure you haven't told us the truth—not nearly the truth. You're not a tourist at all, of course. In fact you've lived in Cairo for several years."

"How can you know that?"

Zagrev shrugged.

"I can admire your stubbornness—up to a point. I can see it is a professional attitude, and I am a professional myself. So is Commander Gamal. The fact of the matter is that in the *felucca* you had something with you. When you saw our boat approaching you dropped that object overboard. Yet it did not sink far, just a few inches on to the surface of the sail. My officer in the stern of the boat saw it there, quietly recovered it and gave it to me."

The gold letters stamped on the cover of the small sodden book Zagrev placed on the desk were already running from the damp, but Rule recognised his passport.

"And what was your function on the staff of the British mission in Cairo?" Zagrev asked.

Rule hesitated; then, as he glanced at Gamal, an elusive memory came forward into sharp focus. He looked at Gamal more intently, and the Egyptian nodded.

"It was at the dedication of the Nasser Memorial Barracks. You met many officers that day, we met only a few official visitors, so it was easy for me to remember you."

"It is natural," Zagrev said, "that Commander Gamal, who was stationed until six months ago in Cairo, should know the name of the British military attaché. Indeed, Colonel Rule is correct, isn't it?"

"I'm not a serving officer at present," Rule said carefully.

"No doubt—yet you are here."

Rule now realised that he was in great danger. It was more than likely that the Russian captain had gone against his orders in stopping to pick up survivors from the *felucca*. Now he had an awkward problem on his hands. If he had not reported Rule's presence aboard *Novgorod* to Moscow, the simplest solution would be to drop him overboard. The risk of permitting him to stay alive would be considerable. He must either be dead, or at best a prisoner. Rule could see himself there were no other possibilities. He could only pray that the matter had not been referred to higher authority, for there was little doubt Moscow would send back orders for what would seem to them the least troublesome course. He took a deep breath.

"I can only tell you that my being here is a complete coincidence. I didn't want to reveal my identity, because I knew it would alarm you if you knew it—but the rest of what I've told you is the plain truth."

"That remains to be seen."

"Surely you can hardly believe that it could have been arranged, with Dr. Marsden critically ill?"

"I accept that she is probably not involved in anything you may be planning, but on your own account your meeting with her was an accident. Now I will credit you with being an efficient operative, Colonel Rule. Such people are not slow to seize opportunities when they arise. What could be a better cover than being with this injured woman? Her dramatic story so easily becomes a part of yours—yet we have only your own word that you were even in Cairo at all at the time of the explosions.

"Colonel Rule—I am not satisfied. Now I will leave it to you to think that over."

Fifteen

MEMORANDUM TO: The President
    FROM: Exec. Assis. (D)

The meeting you requested to advise you prior to the expiry tomorrow of the Soviets' ultimatum on the Middle East took place today between members of the Defense and State Departments and of the staff of the White House.

Basic facts of importance seem to be:

(i) Russian readiness in the Mediterranean theater has increased rapidly, MILSAT and other surveillance apparatus indicating that the continued airlift and naval movements have now shifted a major Russian strike force, with high capability on land, sea, and air, into the Arab countries. The most intensive concentration is in the occupied strip of Sinai and on the opposite bank of the Suez Canal.

(ii) It seems probable that these forces are equipped mainly, if not exclusively, with non-atomic arms. However, there can be little doubt that nuclear weapons have been extensively deployed outside the Mediterranean theater.

(iii) The Suez Canal clearing operation is well advanced, and it may open to traffic within one week.

(iv) British, European, and Japanese determination to remain neutral in any contingency other than actual invasion of their own territory has been maintained, in spite of major diplomatic pressure placed on these governments along the lines you directed.

(v) Almost the whole Russian naval force is at sea in a state of readiness. These units are concentrated mainly in the east Atlantic. The Mediterranean is dominated by our Narwhal type nuclear attack boats and all Russian missile submarines have accordingly left that sea, with most attaching to the Atlantic and Pacific fleets. At least twenty have, however, evaded our search systems and their whereabouts are not known. The most important in this category is one of the two largest and most modern Russian submarines, *Novgorod*, which is armed with twelve Lenin missiles, each with MIRV capability.

Conclusions:

It was the committee's belief that:

(i) in the event of expiry of the ultimatum without agreement on our part to the Amarna proposal, the Soviets will invade Israel forthwith, using only conventional armaments, and so establish the new nation of Amarna in the Palestine territory through conquest.

(ii) that the Soviets plan to avoid using nuclear weapons in the belief that we would not lightly be the first to use them. They know the fears of our European allies, whose extreme vulnerability to atomic attack must be admitted. Hence the Soviets may believe that in a situation where nuclear weapons are not used, they can enjoy a military advantage.

(iii) Russia's eventual and larger aim is to ensure, through the replacement of Israel by a puppet Arab state, dominance in the Middle East. The Suez Canal is being rapidly cleared, and Russian occupation of both banks is plainly designed to give them control over that waterway. Granted this, Russian influence in India, Bangla Desh and Ceylon must increase, while the present *detente* between Russia and China would probably force Pakistan also firmly within the Communist zone of influence.

(iv) Such objectives are very much against the interests of the United States and the free world.

Action to Date:

Since this line of argument is the only one clearly evident to us, we recommend a continued heavy buildup of our own forces in Europe and the Middle East as far as possible, without prejudicing the defense of the United States. Naturally the Soviets know we are making these moves. It is as well they should do so, since it may help to influence them away from the belief that, due to a superiority of non-nuclear arms, they may be able to achieve a swift occupation of Israel without much opposition and perhaps without war.

Recommended Future Action:

It seems to your advisers that this Soviet attitude represents the whole key to the situation. For many decades now it has been Russian policy to probe for weakness, and strike quickly and decisively where this is found. However, there has been a pattern of compromise and withdrawal where these probes have been met by strength and determined opposition. In brief, we believe that too weak an attitude on our part at this stage could be highly dangerous. It is therefore recommended:

(i) that a substantial and balanced U.S. force be moved into Israel from Europe immediately.

(ii) that you issue an immediate statement to the effect that the United States will give all possible aid, using non-nuclear arms only, to Israel, in the event of Soviet invasion of that country.

It is thought that these measures may provide a sufficient deterrent to the Soviets, and induce them at least to extend the period of negotiation.

Extract from news item carried on all transmissions of the Voice of America:

Speaking on a nationwide TV network, the President tonight gravely warned the people of the United States about the Middle East crisis. He revealed that in previous secret negotiations the Soviets had proposed complete dissolution of the state of Israel and the reversion of its lands to the Arab nations.

He said: "I know there is not one person listening to me or watching me tonight who would not agree in their hearts that such a proposal is preposterous and inhuman. Now the Soviets have chosen to issue what they have called an ultimatum to us on this question, and that ultimatum is almost due for expiry. I don't think there'll be many Americans hearing me now who're going to like such talk about ultimatums to us. The United States of America remains the most powerful state in the world, and that position gives us special responsibilities.

"Now as you will all know, for decades our relationship with the Communist world has been one of great delicacy. It has been my duty to continue a policy of doing all we can to see that relationship does not deteriorate beyond a certain point.

"Yet if the Russians are planning blatant aggression against Israel, as I fear they may be, I must warn them that the United States will not desert that small democracy in its hour of need. To me our duty as Americans seems quite clear.

"I have said before, and I will say again, that the United States is well prepared to defend itself, but we are fully aware of the likely consequences of a nuclear war, and we have no wish to see such a holocaust come to pass.

"Hence, should the need arise to help the Israeli people to defend themselves, they may count on the fullest support of American naval, land, and air forces already in that country. These forces are being reinforced hourly, and their deployment into the Sinai area is continuing as I speak. Major United States naval task forces are standing by in the Atlantic and our considerable air-strike and submarine capacity based on Spain has been readied. We have a naval dominance in the Mediterranean.

"Yet I will say as I have also said before, and as my predecessors in this office have said, that we shall not be the first to use nuclear weapons. If we have to fight, it will be with so-called conventional arms only.

"Having spoken thus of our determination to fight if need be, I must make the strongest possible plea to the Soviets not to precipitate a war whose consequences cannot be foreseen. I do not ask them to withdraw from their position. What I do ask is that they postpone their ultimatum for a further thirty days so more mature consideration can be given to their proposals."

Extract from an official news release of TASS:

The Soviet Government and peoples today denounced the move towards war proclaimed by the President of the United States. All over the world peaceful peoples are joining in this denunciation.

The Soviet Government's full statement is:

"The American action in occupying Israel to obstruct its peaceful re-integration into the Arab world is in itself an act of war. Israel has committed great crimes against the Arab peoples, culminating in the explosion of American atomic bombs in Cairo, causing the destruction of that city and millions of its people.

"Many days ago we urged on the rest of the world, and especially the United States, the necessity for a permanent end to the Middle East crisis by correcting the past historical mistake of creating a homeland for the Jews, and the justice of returning those lands to their real owners, the neighbouring Arab states. Within this necessity was recognised the need for tolerance, humanity, and peace, so that it was proposed adequate time and money be provided to make the necessary transfer of those Israelis who might wish to leave. These proposals have been met with aggressive action by the United States, namely, occupation of the claimed lands by American forces.

"The Soviet peoples, the People's Republic of China, the Arab Republic of Egypt, and the other peaceful nations of the world do not, however, lack the means to defend themselves against U.S. aggression. If our peaceful attempt to redress the Middle East balance is thus opposed, we see a moral responsiblity to ensure that the proper course of history is not disturbed.

"Being peace-loving nations, the great peoples of Russia and China have no wish to see the world thrust into a nuclear war, even if through no fault of their

179

own. It is nevertheless evident that some serious action is necessary to persuade the United States away from its reckless and criminal course.

"The navy of the Arab Republic will accordingly launch a nuclear weapon against a satellite nation of the United States if the United States does not agree by the stated time to the peaceful resumption of the Amarna lands.

"The Soviet submarine *Novgorod*, armed with Lenin multiple warhead nuclear missiles, is on loan to the A.R.E. Navy for this purpose. She is now on station in the Pacific, and has been ordered to arm one missile for firing.

"Careful consideration has been given to this matter by all of the socialist democratic nations concerned. They have had recourse to the nomination of such a hostage region with great reluctance and regret, yet have done so only because they feel that the alternatives would place the world in even graver peril.

"The hostage nation is an aggressor of long standing, an eager participant in the war policies of the United States, and one rightly blamed by the peoples of Asia for its share in the suffering brought to the peoples of Indo-China.

"It is a region so located geographically that nuclear fall-out from the explosion should have a minimal effect on innocent neighbours. It contains an urban complex about the same size as Cairo.

"The hostage region nominated is in south-eastern Australia. It lies between longitude 151 and 152 E and latitude 33 and 34 S.

"Unless our terms are met, at midnight Eastern Australian time tomorrow night *Novgorod* will dispatch one missile, armed with three independently targetable eight megaton warheads. These are computed to explode over the city of Sydney and its adjacent industrial complexes, Newcastle and Wollongong.

"It is not our wish to inflict suffering. It is for this reason that we have given the utmost practicable warning—twenty-four hours—so that evacuation of the region can begin at once. It is repeated that this movement of people will not be necessary if the U.S. alters its reckless course towards world war. The fate of these cities, then, is in the hands of Washington."

"Very well, Admiral, you talk," the President of the United States said as soon as he had taken the chair.

"Thank you, Mr. President. There is the obvious first question—can we find this submarine and destroy her? We had early information on *Novgorod* from the 128B MILSAT when she cleared out of the Med—presumably like her sister boats to join the Russian K task force off the coast of Eire. She certainly submerged in the region of the task force a fortnight ago. Two days later it became apparent she was no longer with it. It is now plain that she diverged southward, rounded the Cape of Good Hope, and as we know is on station in the Pacific.

"The Lenin missiles she carries have a maximum range of around two thousand miles, but of course there's no reason why she should be at extreme range for this operation. If I were planning it I'd be a deal closer to Sydney, but not too close. Say anywhere between five hundred and fifteen hundred miles."

He got up, and slashed four pencil lines on to a wall map, enclosing a rough quadrilateral.

"Let's say a million square miles. *Novgorod* is somewhere there, submerged. Her engines are stopped, and she is observing radio silence. Her crew will be under orders not to use any tools that might cause noise, especially on the pressure hull itself, and not to make any other abnormal sound. Every now and again she'll open up her receiving facilities for VLF, to make sure countermanding orders haven't arrived."

He fell silent, then added with careful nonchalance:

"Search vessels and aircraft could pass right over the top of her and never know she was there. That is, they could if there were any. Most of our forces are of course in the Middle East and the European eastern approaches. Nobody had reckoned on anything happening near Australia—gentlemen, in all reason, how could they?"

"Which is an important reason why the Russians chose it," the president said. "Now don't get me wrong. I'm not trying to blame anyone. I agree it's something we could not have foreseen. Even so, we are making some effort to find *Novgorod*, I take it?"

"Everything possible," his services co-ordinator said. "We have every EC121 out of Guam and the Phillipines airborne. We could be lucky, but—"

"Give me odds on that."

"Almost inconsiderable. On our present resources, our chances of taking out *Novgorod* would be of the order of one in a million."

"Thank you. So, we have our first question answered—we cannot stop the submarine firing the missile. Point two—do the Australians have anything down there that could stop it arriving?"

There was silence.

"I want an answer," the President said irritably. "I'll remind you that minutes, even seconds, are important now. Does anyone know?"

"Not real well." The admiral spoke up at last. "There's none of our big stuff down there, not near Sydney anyway. When I was last down around a year ago they had some old radar, some F111s still left, a few missile destroyers and a very obsolete carrier—that's about it. There's nothing that'd have any effect on a Lenin missile. They wouldn't even know it was coming, much less try and stop it."

"Three big cities, right bang on the coast," the president said bitterly. "I wish I could see how this was going to pan out. One thing is sure—we can't afford to give in in a panic. If the people can be gotten out of Sydney in time—and I can't see why not—then we might just leave the Russians to sweat on it. They'd have two choices—one to back down, two to fire the missile."

At that moment the telephone at the president's elbow purred discreetly. Under-Secretary George Clarke, who was sitting next to him, took it up.

His murmured: "It's the Australian Prime Minister," was heard around the table, and caused several people to move restlessly in their chairs.

"Hello," the President said. "Yes, it will be convenient for me to take it. Hello . . . hello . . ."

For thirty long seconds he was silent, then he cleared his throat and said: "Well now, I agree it's just possible they're bluffing, but that's the sort of risk you can't take . . . criminal? Of course it's criminal, but that doesn't alter things . . . never thought it would be you? Why no, never at any time had anyone—"

He stopped abruptly, listening intently. The raised, rapid tones filtered through to other people in the room, although only odd phrases were clearly audible.

"Your people depend on the American alliance?" the President broke in, his own voice raised now. "My God, d'you imagine *we* haven't been thinking about that? Now I'm going to have to tell you some hard facts. Some of them I guess you'll have cottoned on to already ... that's right, but our man puts the chance of finding her in time at one in a million, not one in a thousand ... If the Russians are going to fire that shot, there's no way we can prevent them, there's no way you can stop it arriving. ...

"No, it's not a question of the United States considering Israel more important than Australia—that point doesn't arise. It's a matter of principle ... if we gave in to the Russians over this one there's no telling what, and who, would be next ... You must get on with shifting all your people out, yes, evacuate all three places totally. Half Australia's industry? Yes, I know ... of course not, nothing is definite yet, but evacuation is a wise precaution."

"Any U.S. naval units in Sydney?" the president asked immediately he put down the telephone.

"It's a leave centre for the units helping Suharto put down the Javanese insurgents," someone said. It was the first time this obscure, half-forgotten war had been mentioned in the top national councils for months. "There's bound to be something small in there."

"Have them put to sea with as many people as they can handle, run a ferry service right up to the last minute. Now, to get back to the main issue. I think it's too early to take any decisions. A great deal depends on what happens over the next ten or twelve hours. Every one of you's to stay on here until we make a decision one way or the other. I want constant major intelligence from all possible sources. I want each of you to be in a position to brief us continuously on his own immediate area. We'll meet every hour, on the hour, for as long as necessary, which must also be the shortest time possible. Only people with something significant to say will speak, and I'll be taking a mighty hard view of that. I want facts and sensible deductions from you, not calamity-howling. Thank you, gentlemen . . . George," he added, in a lower voice, to Clarke. "Stop here with me for a while. I need you for a mental punchbag."

He did not look up as the others filed from the room, but began to speak at once to Under-Secretary Clarke, who had been a friend from early in their political careers.

"Think from this starting point, George, please. We are holding an old-fashioned six-gun, a revolver, and we plan to play a game called Russian roulette—you know what that is?"

"I do. A crazy gamble. Just one chamber of the revolver has a cartridge loaded. You spin the magazine so nobody can tell how many times the trigger can be pulled before that shot fires. Each person playing the game puts the gun to his head in turn, and pulls the trigger. When the gun fires, that man dies."

"Right. So off we go, one, two, three, four chambers—still no shot. Now the two players are sitting looking at each other. Which one has the tougher decision?"

Clarke said carefully: "The fifth shot is going to need a great deal of nerve, a lot of courage. But even then the man pulling the trigger the fifth time still has a fifty-fifty chance of living. He still has an option. But after that . . ."

"Number six must back down—or die . . . Now I'm trying to relate this to our present situation, you see it *is* like that, don't you? This is brinkmanship like we've never known it before, George, and it's deadly serious. I don't reckon the Russians are bluffing. They'll go ahead. They'll fire that fifth chamber."

"Why are you so sure?"

"I can't really account for it."

"It's because they're sure we will back down," Clarke said sharply. "If they continue to believe we will back down in the event, they will fire the missile.

If they come to believe we will retaliate with all-out war, then they will not fire it."

The President closed his eyes for a few moments and took a deep breath.

"And you would have me take a decision on that logic?"

He looked directly at Clarke, but his friend would not meet his eyes.

Sixteen

Rule found *Novgorod*'s southward passage almost intolerable. Below the surface, in the artificial light and self-contained climate of the submarine, time crept by as if through one grey, interminable day. Closely confined to the sick-bay, there was nothing to engage his mind except Jean's struggle for life, which he could do nothing to help. During the first two days she remained in a coma, then on the second night Solyikin believed that she would die before morning.

Zagrev came in briefly, late that night. He glanced at Rule, but his whole bearing forbade communication. In spite of his own unhappiness, Rule could not resist watching Zagrev curiously, noticing the hints of his agitation, the quick breathing, the slight tremble of the hands, the clenched fingers. Was it that even now, all these years after the loss of his own family, his emotions had somehow betrayed him into involvement with this stranger who resembled them so much? What horrors, then, did this prospect of a re-enacted death hold for him?

Yet the next morning Jean was marginally improved, and on the fourth day she opened her eyes, looked up at Rule, and smiled. The transfusion appeared to be a success. Her white blood cell count was increasing and with the rapid restoration of the blood-forming mechanisms, her vulnerability to stray infections lessened.

By the sixth day she was able to take food by mouth, and was awake and lucid for lengthy periods. Yet, she complained to Rule, she was now troubled by a curious dualism of consciousness.

"When I'm awake, talking with you like this, only actual things are real," she said. "Then at other times when I'm asleep or almost asleep, I slip across into another world. I'm not just dreaming—it's much more vivid than that. When I was very young it used to happen to me—I'd forgotten about it until . . ." her voice drifted off into silence.

"Is it a pleasant place, that other world?" he prompted her.

She looked up at him silently for a few moments, then shook her head.

"No. Sometimes pleasant things happen in it— you're in it—but it isn't logical. When I was quite small I was taken to see a film of *Alice in Wonderland*. I can still recall my mother carrying me out, so afraid I couldn't move. It was because . . . because nothing fitted. Things happened that weren't normal, like Alice growing bigger and smaller, and I think I was afraid the real world might suddenly turn out to be like that, too. That other place is like that, but it's moving farther away from me all the time. Last night it only came forward for a few minutes."

"You're getting better."

"Am I?"

The thought of recovering seemed to mean little to her. If anything, it brought a note of apprehension to her voice, and for some time afterwards she said nothing, merely staring into vacancy. He felt cut off from her.

The next morning, very early, he heard her cry out, a cry of grief rather than of anger or alarm. The sick-bay was dimly lighted, and they were alone

188

there. When he went to her she had thrown off the sheet, and her brow was creased with pain.

"What is it?" he whispered.

He had to repeat the words several times before she opened her eyes. Then, when she looked at him, they filled with tears.

"The other place again?" he asked.

She nodded.

"We were married. I had a child—a daughter. We were very pleased, until we saw that on her left hand she had six fingers."

A cold hand was laid on his heart.

"We should still love her," he said. "She'd need that even more, wouldn't she?"

Her eyes sought his again.

"You really feel that way? You'd take . . . that risk with me?"

"I haven't any kind of choice," he said humbly. "It's you or nothing at all for me."

"I see. But I was worried—what if there were other things about the girl, things we couldn't know about till later?"

He pressed her hand.

"Go back to sleep."

"It's not so easy. Things like that do happen to people, you know. In Egypt, there are going to be thousands—"

"Stop that!" he said sharply. She looked at him intently.

"Stay with me," she asked.

"Of course." And he stayed by her bed until she drifted off into sleep.

The next morning a similar incident took place, and once again he went to her bedside.

"What's the matter?"

"Oh," she said offhandedly. "It was that girl—the baby. She died. I don't know what caused it."

He said nothing. That day her condition showed

the most marked improvement yet, and there were no more such incidents. From then on her conversation seemed entirely normal and rational.

Zagrev looked up and for the hundredth time saw a fleeting vision of his daughter Sonya. For the slightest fraction of a second it seemed absolutely definite that she was there, but he was left, his heart hammering, his mouth dry, when she disappeared, as though she had merely left the room. Something of her presence remained. Soon she would come in again. He sat down, trembling, and passed a hand over his brow. It was damp with sweat, in spite of the coolness of the air-conditioned atmosphere.

He glanced towards the partition between his cabin and the sick-bay, resisting yet again the urge to go in there, to stare at Jean Marsden—but why? He had no feeling for this stranger, certainly no affection. Yet she aroused in him this dreadful, meaningless fascination, this compulsion to look at her.

The small cabin seemed like a prison. When he looked up, his eyes were compelled to the black button of the firing permissive action link, set beside the small dead eye of its red warning light. He felt his mind shrink from the thought that he might soon have to press that button, for his imagination ranged only too readily beyond that simple act to its monstrous consequences. What was he doing here, he of all men, whose life only two individual deaths had made such an arid hell? He felt a momentary sympathy for Gamal, and shuddered.

Again he read carefully through his final orders. There was nothing in them he had not expected, merely the cold, logical result of his own speculation, his own planning. Moscow had been predictable. It had given its orders, and he was a man under discipline, pledged to obey them. It was a great killer of people, this sense of discipline, he reflected. The mad thought crossed his mind that he could take *Novgorod* to some neutral port, scuttle her, desert— he struck the desk-top with his clenched fist, so violently that the pain shocked him out of these thoughts. Perhaps he should confide in Solyikin, ask him for a tranquilliser or a sedative—but no, that wouldn't do. A commander could not compromise his position, or in any fundamental way share his load of responsibility.

Abruptly Zagrev got up from his chair and splashed a second glass of vodka from the bottle. This he drank, not slowly as usual, but in one gulp, so the neat spirit brought tears to his eyes and a glow to his throat and stomach. He got up and locked his cabin door, something he had never done before. Drinking another glass of vodka came readily to him, as though predestined. He found himself again sitting in his chair, his head down on his hands, gripped by a convulsive wave of sobbing. His heart pounded so he became intensely aware of the throbbing in his fingers' ends.

The emotional storm passed and he felt calmer, eased by it, although physically weakened in some unaccountable way. He replaced the cap on the vodka bottle, washed out the glass and unlocked the door. The sense of panic had receded, but it would come back to take him unawares, to loom up in the background of his dreams.

Was he going mad? Zagrev smiled grimly. No, this was simply his old enemy, with which he had had to fight in the past—too much imagination. This was the ironic price one paid for intelligence, quick perceptions, the power to think and deduce logically, the capacity to be right.

Someone knocked at the door. Zagrev glanced at the clock on the bulkhead. It would be Gamal, with whom he had a regular daily conference at this time.

"Come in," he called. Gamal sat down and looked at Zagrev, who met his glance calmly. He felt quite recovered now, but with the conviction, which he knew to be permanent, that he would never again be the man he had once been. He was not, however, sure that this was weakness, as he had at first thought, but perhaps a consequence of a clearer perception of the meaning of good and evil. The virtues he had once admired, and which others had admired in him—single-mindedness, self-discipline, loyalty, among them—now seemed of less value, perhaps even the instruments of evil itself. It would take him a long time to think this out and now was not the time, so he put these thoughts from his mind.

"Our orders have come," he told Gamal, without particular emphasis. "Here . . . you can read them for yourself."

He watched Gamal read the paper, then give a short grunt of laughter, in which there was no mirth.

"So," Gamal said quietly. "Many lives have been taken, now other lives must pay for them. Soon they will know what it is like, what they did to me, to leave someone with nothing, so he can no longer be himself—"

"That's as it may be," Zagrev said curtly. "But as you'll notice, the Australian cities are hostages. If the Americans will agree to restore the Israeli lands to your people, there is no longer any point in attacking them. In that case, the firing would not take place. Let us hope such is the case."

"I do not so hope," Gamal answered slowly. "It is written that a death must be matched by a death. Can you not see in your mind's eye the bomb exploding over Sydney, flowering out into a great hot sun, its flames licking at the people as though they were ants trapped on a burning log?" He paused and licked his lips. "The Prophet has said in the Holy Koran '. . . the infidels shall be the inmates of the fire, to abide therein eternally . . . for them, garments of fire shall be cut out, the boiling water shall be poured down on their heads . . . all that is in their bowels and their skins shall be dissolved—' "

"Shut up!" Zagrev shouted. There was a tinkling crash. Both men looked down, startled, at the shattered glass the captain had flung against the steel bulkhead.

If they were alone in the sick-bay at that time of evening, as they were on that day, Rule listened to the evening conferences between Zagrev and Gamal. He did this as much to ease his boredom as to obtain information, and had found that if he placed his ear close to the steel wall between him and the captain's cabin, he could hear most of what was said.

On this day it wasn't difficult to draw accurate conclusions about Zagrev's orders from the comments Gamal had made on them, but these seemed at first so startling he needed time to assimilate them.

"What was all the noise about?" Jean asked him.

He hesitated, wondering if he should tell her. She saw this at once, and shook her head.

"I feel quite well . . . please tell me the truth about what's happening . . . I must know, not to know would be worse."

"Very well," he said slowly. "You see, they're preparing to fire the ship's missiles. You realise she carries atomic warheads—the biggest and most destructive submarine-carried bombs the Russians have?"

"I see—more of that," she replied in a whisper. "There's war all over the world, then?"

"Not yet, it seems. We're somewhere off the coast of Australia—a good way off, I'd say, but the east coast cities would be in range. The Russians are using Sydney to force the Americans to agree to an ultimatum. It involves a handover of Israeli territory to the Arabs . . . if the Americans won't permit this, then Sydney will be attacked with an atomic weapon in retaliation."

"But what's Australia got to do with Israel? We've never done anything there, never interfered in the Middle East."

"Heaven knows," he said. "It sounds insane—but take my word for it, the military planning of the nuclear age is insane. Once you penetrate the jargon of any modern book on strategy it all boils down to sheer, illogical horror. Megadeaths, for example. One megadeath means the inevitable, premeditated killing of a million people, from babies taking their first breath to the aged. The textbooks already list numbers of megadeaths regarded as "acceptable" in the case of war."

"People don't know about it," she said.

"Because they don't want to know. You'll find books like that, perfectly serious factual studies, in any large public library. As for the choice of Australia—it is a logical enough development of that strategy as a last step before all-out war under conditions where Russian and American nuclear potential is evenly balanced.

"For Russia to strike at the United States, or *vice versa*, would be to invite ultimate retaliation. The obvious solution then is to strike at a weak, far distant ally, or to hold that ally to ransom. After that it's only a matter of selecting the most appropriate target area, and in terms of this mad logic Australia pretty well selects itself, doesn't it? Because of the world division of opinion over the Vietnam war and now the Indonesian business Australia's tied up in with the United States, plenty of honest, well-intentioned people everywhere would have been conditioned to accept the idea of a possible attack on it, even if not to approve of it.

"Then there's the remoteness from Europe, from

194

Russia, from the United States itself. Most people have few scruples about suffering in places they don't know. The great achievement of television has been to insulate people emotionally from the sufferings of others—that would help the acceptability of an attack on Sydney.

"Next there's self-interest, the feeling of relief, admitted or not, that if a thermo-nuclear bomb has to explode somewhere, far better for it to be over a lightly-populated country so remote the fall-out could not possibly affect the northern hemisphere. Also, it's certain the Australian cities are sitting ducks, impossible to defend against this sort of attack."

"The whole idea is ghastly. It can't happen," she said. "The Americans won't let it happen. We've always stood by them."

"Of course they'd stop it if they could. But could they? You can be sure the Russians have taken good care to see *Novgorod* moved in complete secrecy. Submerged, she'd be almost impossible to find. She doesn't even have to surface to fire her missiles. You'd noticed the engines had stopped?"

"It's much quieter."

"We'll be on the firing station. Now it's only a matter of time, while the ultimatum runs out."

"If only we could do something . . ."

"But what? Supposing I could get past that guarded door on the other side of the captain's cabin, what then? I don't know how the firing's carried out, except that the final action is controlled by the captain himself—"

"In the next cabin." She completed the sentence for him.

"Yes."

"Then don't be stupid. All you could possibly hope for would be to delay matters for a little while, and it would cost you your life. My God, doesn't it mean something now just to stay alive—even if it's only for days, or weeks, or months? What'll they do with us—afterwards?"

"There's no telling. I suppose the ship'll go back to Russia."

"If they make the attack on Sydney, there'll be a world war."

"Perhaps, if it had been an American or a European city. I can see that the Russians would have thought out that point very carefully—that's why they chose Sydney. It's a nicely calculated risk, but on the whole I think the United States might just have to accept the situation, rather than take steps that would cause the destruction of how many . . . twenty, thirty, a hundred cities? Somewhere it has got to stop."

"It's as well C.I.A. waited to come to me over this," the President said irritably as he passed a document across the table to Clarke.

"What is it?"

"They want to kidnap an Admiral Komorov and his wife from their apartment in Moscow. We have information that Komorov knows *Novgorod*'s position."

"Do we have people in Moscow able to do that?"

"We have people in Moscow who could do it," the President replied grimly. "They wouldn't live long, but it would be possible. On the face of it, the idea doesn't seem a bad one, but it won't stand close examination. What d'you think?"

He stared at Clarke.

"You're right," Clarke said almost at once. "Supposing Komorov did crack—the Russians would be alarmed, they might well advance their plans. Also, there'd be no way at all of knowing in time whether Komorov had told the truth."

"So I thought. It's tempting, but much too risky. See the idea's killed, will you?"

Clarke turned to a telephone.

"Come in," the President said to the secretary who stood diffidently by the door. "What is it?"

"Some information has just come in from defense coordination. General Maxwell believes your meeting ought to reconvene at once."

"I wanted us to meet on the hour. There's twenty-five minutes to go yet."

"He says this is too important to wait."

"If he says so, then it must be—it had better be. Get them back in here then."

"Well, General Maxwell, let's hear it," the President said as soon as the meeting had assembled.

The general took a deep breath and plunged directly into his subject.

"The latest MILSAT orbits over Soviet Russia indicate some surprising and alarming things. At the moment we have only the early photographs relayed back by the satellite, but these show clearly that there is an immense and well-organised movement of people out of a number of the main cities. This is happening in Moscow, Leningrad, Kiev, Kharkov, and Baku, also in some of the big industrial cities back of the Urals.

"There are huge convoys of buses and trucks on all the roads. They're crowded with traffic, but it's orderly and it keeps moving. Every railway wagon and carriage the Russians have, and every locomotive, must be in use, all carrying people. Our lowest-level photographic satellite sent some good clear pictures and part of one of these we have blown up real big and printed. This is it."

He passed a number of glossy, still-damp prints around the table.

"It's coarse and grainy because of the enlargement and the speed of the film, but you can see the line of trucks. It's a bit hard to identify what's in them. One might imagine they were animals, but our experts on photographic analysis assure me they're people all right. We did a rough estimate on the numbers carried by this particular train, which was leaving Kiev. The people are being given standing room only—roughly one hundred and twenty to an open freight-car. There are forty cars—that makes about five thousand people."

"Then the Russians are taking this mighty seriously," the President commented. "This is happening in all the big Russian cities?"

"Not all, but most—especially the biggest centres of population. Those five places I mentioned have a total population of around sixteen millions."

"Even if they make people stand up in freight-cars, they can't hope to shift that number in a day."

"I should add that just because these are the first pictures we've had, it doesn't necessarily mean the evacuation's just started. Most of the Eurasian land-mass had medium to heavy cloud cover all yesterday and part of the day before. These are the first clear pictures we've had for thirty-eight hours. We did have some infra-red reaction during yesterday and last night, but our analysts considered that to be most likely military traffic."

The President raised his eyebrows slightly.

"Their orders don't give them scope for conjecture," Maxwell explained patiently.

"Just a moment, before you go on," the President said, ignoring this last comment. "I'd like to absorb what you've told us and think about it. Maybe we should start evacuating our cities too, if they've started. Civil defense have plans made for that, of course?"

His suggestion was at first received in silence. Finally George Clarke, to whom it so often fell to make the less welcome points, replied: "There are certainly such plans along broad lines for some cities, but it'd be difficult to get them moving in . . . what have we? . . . less than twenty hours now. It's a different story in Russia. There not so many people have automobiles. Everything's geared to a big public transport system, especially rail. That makes it easier for them to move people fast. Also, the orderly way the evacuation's proceeding suggests it's going to a carefully worked out, possibly pre-rehearsed plan. Don't you think so, general?"

"Yes, sir," Maxwell replied. "All the evidence shows it's probably the most fantastically large exercise in logistics the world's ever seen. Ivan doesn't do things by halves. Then of course the people there are better organised than ours. When they're told to do something, they do it."

"That's a point we needn't take up time with," the President commented mildly. "What else?"

"Look next at this picture. It's also just a sample of what we're getting in all the time, from the Ural industrial cities not actually being evacuated and the major Russian I.C.B.M. sites—all prime targets on our N.S.T.L.* These places show no evidence of population evacuation at all. Instead, these things have turned up over the last two days."

There was no doubt this time what the prints showed. Staggered double rows of needle-nosed missiles pointed to the sky, mounted on individual launchers. Closer examination showed associated batteries of smaller missiles and a number of heavy, enclosed trucks, many of which carried circular radar antennae on squat, roof-mounted towers.

"A.B.M. deployment," the President said softly.

"Yes, and a powerful lot of it, more than we'd ever believed possible, both long and short range anti-missile missiles, with tracking radar and computers in

*National Strategic Target List.

those big closed trucks. And every rocket sits on a mobile launcher. They've built all this stuff secretly somewhere, under cover, so we'd underestimate their defense capability."

The President nodded.

"We have certainly done that," he remarked, looking steadily at the C.I.A. director, who squirmed in his seat. "I'd like to have thought we'd got wind of this sooner through our own intelligence, instead of all those expensive games we've been playing in Laos and Cambodia. However, we'll not waste time on that now. The point is that they'll stop one hell of a lot more of our I.C.B.M.s than we can stop of theirs—also we'd be shooting at empty cities while they fired at cities full of people."

Maxwell nodded.

"So," the president insisted. "If it came to all-out war, we'd be mauled much more severely than they would?"

"Especially in terms of civilian casualties," Maxwell said. "That is the position."

"I see." He sat for a full minute, brooding, while they all watched him. "Well, there's little point in beating dead horses," he continued at last. "But the fact is that while we've been occupied elsewhere, this is what the Russians have been doing. Every time one of our choppers is lost in Laos or Thailand or Indonesia, every time we drop a bomb, the Russians get that much ahead of us, somewhere, somehow. It's a simple matter of production. Now we have to pay.

"All I can hope is that the price-tag won't be too big. On that score there's just one thing more, I believe, you can do for me—get down on your knees and pray for some way out that won't lose us too much face."

Seventeen

Nine thousand miles away to the south-west two high-pressure atmospheric systems had developed off the east Australian coast. These would have dispersed rapidly and without lasting effects under the normal weather conditions for early summer, but this time an unusual combination of circumstances caused them to remain stationary, while increasing in size and intensity.

Strong, humid easterlies began to blow on to most of the New South Wales coast from the pressure ridge that built up between them. The weather in the Tasman and southern Pacific was already warm, causing the east winds to breed huge masses of dense, heavily-laden cloud. This low-flying cloud, so black as to appear almost purple, drove wave after wave of violent rainstorms on to the land.

Within hours the rain from this freak weather represented the highest daily total in Sydney for more than a year. By dawn, when people began getting up and listening to the urgent warnings that had displaced all other radio programmes, more rain had been recorded at the Sydney Weather Bureau, which forecast continued heavy falls during the day. Every quarter hour or so storms so heavy as to blot out all visibility alternated with heavy drizzle.

Earlier in the night police had begun working outwards from all suburban stations, going from door to door to warn as many people as possible of the order to evacuate the city. Public servants were called from their beds to dial all numbers in the Sydney directory and read a standard warning to anyone who answered. Signals were sounded on sirens, factory horns, hooters, and ships' whistles.

By dawn these measures had been operating for three hours. The main road outlets already carried very heavy traffic which, however, was still moving. Police at roadblocks stopped and sent back all incoming traffic, so the full width of the roads could be used in the one direction. The normal morning train services carrying workers to the city were cancelled. Instead, all available rolling stock had been organised into evacuation trains moving outwards along the northern, southern, and western lines, stopping at every station until theoretically they were full. Several of these trains cleared the outer suburbs only half-full, due partly to the weather, but even more to haste of dispatch, aimed at getting the trains back as soon as possible to shift more people.

By dawn about two hundred thousand of Sydney's three millions were on their way out of the city. It was after that, when people woke up and heard their radios, that such great pressure was thrown on to road transport outlets that they broke down. People who went to the railway stations after daylight found that all the evacuation trains had already left. None would be back for a second trip for at least four hours and most later than that, since it was necessary for those taking the northern and southern lines to go well beyond Wollongong and Newcastle, where independent evacuations were already operating.

The logical route for the evacuation of Sydney, and that relied on most heavily by the planners, was the only other major rail outlet, the western line through the Blue Mountains to the inland. The first four trains, travelling at speeds well above normal, cleared the city safely and reached the end of the electrified line at Lithgow, eighty miles inland and three thousand feet up in the mountains.

It was the fifth train, carrying nearly two thousand people, that jumped the tracks at the eastern approach to the high-level bridge over the swollen Nepean River, which flows between the Blue Mountains and the coastal plain. The cause of this accident was not known, but it was probably due to dangerous overcrowding of the carriages, combined with high speed.

Travelling at more than sixty miles an hour, the train plunged on to the main structure of the bridge. When it was about a third of the way across the locomotive smashed through the steel side of the bridge, dragging the carriages after it into the fast-running, muddy floodwaters below. Only in the last three carriages, which were derailed on the eastern bank, were there any survivors.

Most serious of all was the destruction of both rail tracks and one side of the bridge—damage so extensive that repair within days, perhaps even weeks, was out of the question.

The Nepean, fed by scores of mountain streams, continued to rise catastrophically. Ten miles downstream the lesser-used of the two highways across the river was cut as the low-level bridge at Yarramundi went under water. The last vehicle to get across was a bus. A car close behind it was swept away and its occupants drowned. After that nobody else attempted the crossing.

It now became only a matter of time until the only remaining escape route to the west, the Great Western Highway through Penrith, was cut by floodwaters. This happened just before half past ten. However, it now ceased to be important whether or not the highway was open, for inside Sydney itself every main road was jammed with lines of traffic which had ceased to move.

When it became obvious that the rail services could not cope, those people shrewd enough to think carefully, in good health and unencumbered with small children, began to walk away from the city immediately. These, however, were a very small percentage. Most people thought only of collecting a few of their most valued possessions, and using the family car.

Virtually every car in Sydney was soon on the roads, creating traffic conditions without precedent. Most of these cars were overloaded and many more towed trailers, due to the nuclear exclusion clauses introduced by all Australian insurance companies in household policies in 1967. People who knew that they would get no compensation for loss of their effects tried to take as much as possible with them.

Probably five per cent of these vehicles were in no condition to keep going through the hours of low-gear driving and torrential rain, and possibly as many more simply ran out of petrol before they could clear the suburbs. For an hour the police kept the traffic moving slowly, by towing or pushing stalled cars over banks, into gradens, and anywhere else they could be shifted. Then the sheer volume of vehicles disabled by empty fuel-tanks, damp ignition, burned-out clutches, and overheating became so great the towing teams could no longer get near the points of obstruction, much less clear them.

It was then that road traffic stopped moving, law and order ceased to apply and panic took over.

"How many people will be left in Sydney at midnight?" the American President asked the Australian Ambassador, Sir Robert Mudick, who was pale-faced, his eyes smudged with fatigue.

"I only have rough estimates. It's been much easier to deal with Newcastle and Wollongong—they're smaller, and closer to suitable evacuation areas. You'll understand that these places lie north and south of Sydney. To the west—"

"Pardon me," the President interrupted. "I didn't ask for a geography lesson. You haven't answered my question."

"I'm sorry. Probably two million people would still be within the major casualty area by tonight."

"How are you defining that?"

"Within thirty miles north and south of Sydney, and forty miles to the west. But if the east wind keeps up the position could get much worse—very much worse. We're told the weather influences that brought on this rain and the easterly air stream are still not moving. The forecasters say the pattern may hold for a number of days yet.

"If that happens the wind would carry the fall-out directly into the populated areas of the near-west. During persistent rain we understand that the concentration of radio-active particles reaching the ground quickly can be very much increased. All the water supplies would be contaminated, almost at once."

The President drummed his fingers on the desk.

"I understand. Most of the people you've managed to get out of Sydney are in that near-west region?"

"Yes—as well as the normal population. The fall-out could affect as many as another million people."

The President felt there was little to say. He looked for a few moments at Mudick in silence, then got up from his chair.

"Thank you for coming. Tell your prime minister I'll give this the most serious and urgent consideration, and I'll keep him informed through you."

Mudick had not risen.

"Is that all I can tell him?"

"You have relatives in Sydney yourself?" the President asked quietly.

"My daughter, her husband, and their two children. They're in Bellevue Hill—one of the eastern suburbs. They'll be the hardest of all to get away from."

"I'm sorry. I'll do what I can, but you'll understand that for the moment I can't promise what that will be. You're a veteran diplomat, Sir Robert—we've been good friends for quite a time. You must see that I have . . ." his voice trailed off and then he said, more firmly ". . . responsibilities. What would you do if you were in my position?"

Mudick went on staring at him for a few moments, then shook his head and got up from his chair.

"God knows," he said heavily.

The President chose to take this literally.

"Probably," he said thoughtfully. "In all sincerity, Sir Robert, I wish there were some way He could tell me."

But even before the door had closed behind Mudick the President was thinking about what he had to do. He closed his eyes in an effort to shut the present crisis out of his mind and allow his imagination to range far into the future.

How was it possible to judge the remote consequences of one's actions, he wondered? Because of what he might do, there could be, not so far ahead, a Communist world. How much might the future depend on the simple fact that an elderly man—himself—had had a long and tiring day? He tried his best to be detached, and honest with himself. Was it best, as he knew the generals would advise, simply to let the ultimatum expire? Perhaps then the Russians would flinch from the action they had threatened. If they did not, and the attack on the Australian cities took place, an American Poseidon submarine could "take out" a city on the other side—Hanoi, perhaps?

No, that was too close to the Chinese border, it had better be—

"I am not a wicked man," he suddenly said to himself, distinctly and aloud.

He got to his feet and began to pace restlessly around the room, finally stopping before a glass-doored case near the window. He began looking at the books, not the new ones put there because someone thought he ought to read them, but the older, faded ones, the friends of his youth and early manhood. He took down a big, well-used copy of *Walden*, printed years ago by the Peter Pauper Press at Mount Vernon, and glanced at the lithographs, in dark and light green, by Aldren Watson.

". . . if one designs to construct a dwelling-house," he read, "it behooves him to exercise a little Yankee shrewdness, lest after all he finds himself in a workhouse, a labyrinth without a clue, a museum, an almshouse, or a splendid mausoleum instead."

The President smiled. He idly flipped over a few more pages. ". . . the cost of a thing is the amount of what I will call life that is required to be exchanged for it, immediately or in the long run."

He snapped the book shut, and put it carefully back on the shelf. He would like to get the decision over, go to bed, then tomorrow get out into the country somewhere, fishing. The weather in Sydney was plainly most opportune. One might even see the hand of God in it. His thoughts racing on rapidly, he judged that it would be best not to appeal to the Russians to desist on humanitarian grounds—that would only make him appear all the more the appeaser history might well judge him to be.

At least it would be plain that he had had his reasons. Also, even more importantly to himself, he could go on living with his conscience, that so grave a tyrant, taskmaster, and perplexer of decent Americans. He would not, of course, be a hero to posterity—and what politician did not nurse that secret hope? He surrendered it with brief pangs.

Outside they were waiting for him.

"Well," he told them dispassionately, "I believe we have lost the battle but, I trust, not the war. What we need now is time, and I must buy it as I can. That means accepting the Russian conditions."

Novgorod lay motionless under a sunny Pacific sea, well east of the rain influences, during the remainder of that day. The order cancelling the firing came with evening, and with it instructions to remain on station until midnight, as a safeguard against the small but actual risk of American duplicity.

In the missile compartment the big Lenin rocket remained armed, its guidance system and computers tirelessly maintaining their aim on the targets, while on the other side of the world Israeli military units stood by as the Russian columns moved into Sinai. There were isolated points of resistance, which were soon eliminated. In general the Israelis, who had had adversity for a teacher, were realists, and squarely faced the hard truth that after weeks of mounting fear, world opinion was now overwhelmingly for any steps that would avert war.

Aboard *Novgorod*, Zagrev shared for a time this feeling of a relief so great as to be almost unbearable, until it was replaced by elation. Already a message of congratulation had come from Moscow. Zagrev's strategy had had the ultimate merit of success, and could well have altered the major course of history. His name would be remembered by his people.

It was with such thoughts that Zagrev composed himself for sleep, the first real rest he had had for more than two weeks. Drowsily his mind slipped back to the time when, as a little boy, on cold nights, he had felt reassured by the warm, cavelike security of his bed. Tonight he felt like that again. His dreams carried him back to the time of his youth, which he recalled now as a happy one, when days were long and peaceful, the sun shone brighter, and there was not yet any heavy burden of experience and responsibility.

In his dream it was dawn—a cold, clear morning of late autumn, with the light spreading slowly into a calm, frosty world. This dawn was tranquil, its colours muted and unemphasised. The light gradually increased in intensity and then, suddenly, the sun rose, not with the gentle amber glow he had expected, but vivid and blood-red, so it cast a ghastly scarlet over the mild landscape. With the coming of this violent sunrise he also felt a sudden apprehension, the acute return of fear and tension.

He woke with a start.

The red warning light beside the permissive action link firing button was glowing in the darkness. For a few seconds he merely stared at it, his mind desperately clearing itself of the tatters of his dream so it could return to this incredible, monstrous crisis. The circuits of that lamp had been checked, double and treble-checked. If it were on, there could only be one reason: The firing button in the weapons control compartment had been pressed, and was in contact.

Zagrev got up in one quick movement and felt for the switch of the reading-lamp clipped to the head of his bed. As the room flooded with light he heard a soft laugh. Gamal was sitting in the chair near the door.

"So, my captain," he said. "For all these days I have listened to you and watched you. You thought it was Zagrev who had power over life and death but it is me, after all, Gamal, for I am here as the messenger of God."

Zagrev felt a surge of anger. He moved forward,

then stopped as Gamal lifted the gun that lay in his lap.

"No closer."

"Put down that gun," Zagrev said quietly. "If you do so, I will consider the incident closed. But if you give more trouble I shall have you arrested for mutiny, and when we get to Vladivostok you will be executed by a firing squad."

"How can the incident be closed?" Gamal asked mildly. "But of course you are also an infidel, so you cannot understand that I could be the messenger of God—that if I succeed, as I shall—the results of my success must be his will. For, as it says in the third *sura* of the Holy Book . . . '. . . no one can die, except by God's permission. . . .' As for arresting me, why, no help can come to you, for we have killed the guard on the damage control door and it is clipped shut on this side."

"Tell me what happened at the missile firing room."

"There is no harm in telling you. Maif and my other people are holding it. They went quietly there, with guns we had hidden with more care than the ones you found. They did not have to kill the duty crewman, only the man at your door was unreasonable. There we used a knife, quietly. So, you can see that all has gone well and easily. That is because Allah himself smiles on the plan he placed in my mind.

"Only one thing remains. You yourself must press the second button here, in this room, so the rocket will be fired. So the great purpose will be achieved. That is something infidels have never understood, but which our faith teaches us again and again—that vengeance is a virtue, having merit of itself. Allah demands it! The dead of Cairo, my wife—"

"Gamal!"

Zagrev strove to concentrate all the authority he could muster into his words. "Recognise that you are mentally sick. You're in need of treatment. It's not your fault. Put down the gun—now—and I'll call Solyikin. He'll give you something to make you sleep and when you wake, you'll feel better.

"Now listen to me! We have succeeded. We are victorious. When we reach Vladivostok we'll be greeted as heroes. And I can do more for you—much more. I'll recommend that you be appointed governor of one of the Amarna provinces—Tel Aviv itself! Life will be very good for you, you'll have power, comfort, authority, prestige—yes, and Jew-girls. For God's sake *listen*, Gamal. There's no reason now to fire the missile. If it's fired millions of innocent people will die—people who now believe they're safe. Then war is certain to follow at once—within minutes the rockets will be crossing the Atlantic. Who can say how long and how far such a war would go?"

Gamal smiled sadly.

"You are well-meaning, but your thoughts are wrong. The war against the infidel can never end, no, not while there is even one of them alive, or any that have refused the true faith. It would be possible for me to press the button myself, but it is written that you should do so. Do it now."

"Gamal! Stop and think about this, for a few more minutes. Just for long enough for us to discuss it quietly—have some vodka—"

"There can be no reason for more talk. I will count to five. If you have not by then pressed the button, I must fire, first at your left arm. One, two, three. Four—"

The echoes of the shot slammed around the steel walls of the cabin. Zagrev looked down, dazed with shock, at the blood surging from the smashed muscle just above his left wrist. The heavy calibre bullet had cut an artery as well as tearing a gaping wound.

Gamal's voice came again, shaking slightly.

"You are foolish, Zagrev. It grieves me to deal with you so. We've been good friends after all. You have been kind to me. If in the end I must kill you, then I myself will fire the missile. Think, it remains possible for you to live, and in the end everything will be the same, except that you will be alive, instead of dead. You are afraid, Zagrev—I can see it in your face. I don't want to kill you, yet once more, if you don't obey, I must injure you."

As he started to count again, Zagrev saw the handle of the door behind Gamal begin to turn slowly. Just as Gamal fired, Zagrev flung himself sideways. The shot screeched past, clanged off the wall, then ricocheted before it buried itself in the mattress of the bed behind him.

The door opened.

Zagrev saw Rule, an indistinct figure through the smoke and the bloody veil of pain. Rule's right arm closed around Gamal's throat and tightened viciously, his left hand groping for the gun. Again a shot bellowed out. The two men struggled. Dizzy with loss of blood and pain, Zagrev could not move. From the other side of the damage control door came the heavy clang of steel on steel—blows of a sledgehammer or an axe.

Gamal released the gun, leaving it in Rule's hand as he broke free and jumped to his feet. Zagrev's eyes focused briefly on Gamal as he ran for the firing button, beside which the baleful red light still glowed.

"Shoot him!" Zagrev heard his own cracked voice screaming.

Rule fired without hesitation, as if on an order, at the back of Gamal's neck. Instantly Gamal changed from a living man into a dummy, whose head lolled ridiculously sideways. Yet his outflung hand continued to move.

Zagrev felt his spine prickle, his mind dissolve into horror, as the contracting fingers struck for the button.

Somewhere in the ship a siren sounded. After a few moments came a dull concussion. *Novgorod* moved uneasily in the water.

THE ELECTION, by Sherwin Markman. What happens when an exciting presidential election is tied, and the final decision is thrown into the House of Representatives. Heightening the complications and tensions, too, are the simultaneous riots of black militants across the country. America is in chaos! The pivotal figure in this melee is Stu Brady, a young assistant press secretary. Stu becomes the liaison man between the major candidates, as scandal and intrigue come to the boiling point. An election you'll never forget! **P100—$1.50**

CLASH OF DISTANT THUNDER, by A. C. Marin. A spy story you'll find difficult to put down; impossible to forget. The spy, Dr. John Wells. His assignment, to find a missing informant in Paris. This misplaced agent may have defected or may have been a double agent right along. Or he may have been loyal—but has been caught and silenced. Wells is the hunted as well as the hunter, from Paris to Switzerland and Italy. A wild chase of shadows and suspense. **P064—95¢**

the Executioner

The gutsiest, most exciting hero in years. Imagine a guy at war with the Godfather and all his Mafioso relatives! He's rough, he's deadly, he's a law unto himself — nothing and nobody stops him!

THE EXECUTIONER SERIES by DON PENDLETON

Order		Title	Book #	Price
_____	# 1	WAR AGAINST THE MAFIA	P401	$1.25
_____	# 2	DEATH SQUAD	P402	$1.25
_____	# 3	BATTLE MASK	P403	$1.25
_____	# 4	MIAMI MASSACRE	P404	$1.25
_____	# 5	CONTINENTAL CONTRACT	P405	$1.25
_____	# 6	ASSAULT ON SOHO	P406	$1.25
_____	# 7	NIGHTMARE IN NEW YORK	P407	$1.25
_____	# 8	CHICAGO WIPEOUT	P408	$1.25
_____	# 9	VEGAS VENDETTA	P409	$1.25
_____	#10	CARIBBEAN KILL	P410	$1.25
_____	#11	CALIFORNIA HIT	P411	$1.25
_____	#12	BOSTON BLITZ	P412	$1.25
_____	#13	WASHINGTON I.O.U.	P413	$1.25
_____	#14	SAN DIEGO SIEGE	P414	$1.25
_____	#15	PANIC IN PHILLY	P415	$1.25
_____	#16	SICILIAN SLAUGHTER	P416	$1.25
_____	#17	JERSEY GUNS	P417	$1.25
_____	#18	TEXAS STORM	P418	$1.25
_____	#19	DETROIT DEATHWATCH	P419	$1.25

AND MORE TO COME . . .

TO ORDER

Please check the space next to the book/s you want, send this order form together with your check or money order, include the price of the book/s and 25¢ for handling and mailing to:

PINNACLE BOOKS, INC. / P.O. Box 4347
Grand Central Station / New York, N.Y. 10017

☐ CHECK HERE IF YOU WANT A FREE CATALOG

I have enclosed $_____ check_____ or money order_____
as payment in full. No C.O.D.'s

Name_____

Address_____

City_____ State_____ Zip_____
(Please allow time for delivery)